WALLFLOWERS

ELIZA ROBERTSON

WALLFLOWERS

B L O O M S B U R Y
LONDON • NEW DELHI • NEW YORK • SYDNEY

First published in Great Britain 2015

Bloomsbury Publishing Plc
50 Bedford Square
London
WC1B 3DP

www.bloomsbury.com

Bloomsbury is a trademark of Bloomsbury Publishing Plc

Bloomsbury Publishing, London, New Delhi, New York and Sydney

A CIP catalogue record for this book is available from the British Library

ISBN 978 1 4088 5679 6

10 9 8 7 6 5 4 3 2 1

Printed and bound in Great Britain by CPI Group (UK) Ltd, Croydon CR0 4YY

For Toad, Bear, and Moose

CONTENTS

Who Will Water the Wallflowers? 1

Ship's Log 19

My Sister Sang 39

Worried Woman's Guide 57

Nightwalk 79

Where have you fallen, have you fallen? 91

Roadnotes 111

L'Étranger 131

Electric Lady Rag 143

We Are As Mayflies 165

Missing Tiger, Camels Found Alive 185

Sea Life 205

Thoughts, Hints, and Anecdotes Concerning Points of Taste and the Art of Making One's Self Agreeable: A Handbook for Ladies 225

Good for the Bones 241

Here Be Dragons 251

Slimebank Taxonomy 265

We Walked on Water 285

Who Will Water the Wallflowers?

The day before the flood, the girl slices lemons into a wide-mouthed mason jar. She has been reading about storage devices in the sunroom. Jars will replace Tupperware, she reads, for leftovers. They will store tulips, sourdough starter, kombucha. Ms. Feliz must have read the article too, because these vessels fill her larder. Crystal-cut pots of marmalade line the bottom shelf, and above that, quarts of beans and crumpled tongue chipotles. They appear to the girl as display cases. She expects to find a flask of dead bees on the shelf, or water beetles. A Mesozoic crab. The girl's larder contains no such jars. Her mother buys items in cardboard boxes. Often, the boxes remain in the cupboard long after they have been emptied. Neither she nor her mother like to untuck the seal and flatten the cases into bright cards of recycling. Their hands navigate around them instead. They rattle each box of Kraft Dinner or Hamburger Helper before they lift it from the shelf.

Ms. Feliz left last week for her time-share in Palm Springs. She is paying the girl ten dollars a day to pet her cat,

Cha-Cha, and water the lemon tree. She has left a pint of unpeeled eggs in the fridge. When Ms. Feliz baby-sat the girl ten years ago, she prepared eggs at every meal: a soft egg with toast soldiers for breakfast; hard-boiled with cantaloupe for lunch. At dinner, she carved the eggs into triangles and tossed them with potatoes.

Boiled eggs for you, Ms. Feliz wrote on the checklist she stuck to the fridge. *Feed the spares to the raccoons.*

The week the girl cat-sits for Ms. Feliz, the rain starts. Fat toads fall from the sky and fill the hanging geranium pots. The soil cannot contain it; water courses over the thin terra-cotta bowls like open mouths. In the kitchen, she listens to the rain stamp on the roof while she carves lemons. Ms. Feliz grows the lemon tree in an earthenware pot on the counter. Thirteen fruit nipple from the leaves and bend the branches into the sink. The acid bites her fingertips as she works, revealing all her nicks and holes—a paper-cut on her thumb, a torn nail bed. After she quarters two lemons, she washes her hands and pours cold water into the jar.

Across the street, Mr. Bradley pulls his Mazda into his driveway and emerges from the driver's seat. A folded umbrella swings on his wrist. She often passes her neighbour on the walk home from school. She knows his stance from the bottom of the road—stiffly stacked, like a candlestick. He wears a suit jacket while he tosses a stick for his dog. Despite the office clothes, she wonders if he works from home. He is always there. She steps outside to help her mother with the groceries, or call Ms. Feliz's cat, and he appears on cue, in ironed slacks and flip-flops to collect the mail. His wife is a thin woman who wears needle-heeled shoes and cranberry jumpsuits. She works in town, the girl thinks. Her heels click down the driveway every morning.

The girl winds the metal ring over her lemon water. She leaves the jar in the fridge and removes a tin of Cha-Cha's cat food. He hasn't come inside yet, which is unusual during such rain. He is a delicate breed—a Turkish angora. This rain could wash him away. She spoons the pâté into his dish, then opens the front door. The rain chutes off the porch eaves. Even the roof troughs overflow.

"Cha-Cha!" she calls.

Across the street, Mr. Bradley reopens his car door, then shuts it again. Rain fills his collar. His hair drips down the thin line of his suit.

"Oh, hi," he shouts from his driveway. "Didn't see you there."

"Hey Mr. Bradley."

"Ms. Feliz working you to the bone again?"

"Just feeding her cat."

"How's school?"

"It's fine."

"Learn something?"

She never knows what to say to that. He asks her every day. To avoid replying, she crouches to the porch step and scans the cedar shrubs.

"Cha-Cha!" she calls again.

When she stands, Mr. Bradley hasn't moved.

"Today we watched a movie on geysers," she offers.

He smiles through the rain. The water spiders his eyebrows.

"I know a joke about geysers," he says.

Cha-Cha appears from the shadows and tears between her heels.

"It probably wouldn't be appropriate."

The wet shag of Cha-Cha's tail rounds the hallway corner. She turns after him.

"Got to go, Mr. Bradley. Good night."

The designers built every home in Copper Waters off the same floor plan. Two bedrooms, one bath. A row of cedar shrubs separates each driveway, and behind the shrubs, one square cartwheel of grass. To identify her house without door numbers, she must count the lots from the entrance. Or recognize the parked cars. Or estimate her *x* and *y* coordinates on the Apple Crescent parabola. All the streets in the subdivision are named after fruit trees. Once, she conducted a study on suburban nomenclature for her Career and Personal Planning class. She researched the names of behavioural health facilities, rehabilitation centres, and ready-home subdivisions. Sandy Gallop, Lavender Hill, Arbutus Grove. The titles were indistinguishable.

Both her mother and Ms. Feliz left their rooms as sold. The decorator painted them a starchy colour, like blended potatoes. Only the bathrooms were spared, and these became her favourite spaces. An artist stencilled plants on the walls with such care the girl can identify them in her *Farmer's Almanac*. Irises spring behind the taps, and fists of hyacinth. Wisteria fills the tub. A spray of lilac peels off the wall and nods into the toilet.

The girl enters the bathroom after she finds Cha-Cha. Tonight more than ever, she feels the heat of the photosynthesis, the roots on the wall silently sucking. She fetches the comb from the soap dish and joins the cat in the living room. On a hand towel behind the door, a peony spreads its petals and belches.

The fur of a Turkish angora resembles feathers, each hair free to lift from the rest, sensitive to breeze, gathered in a pearly crest around the sternum. Sometimes she expects Cha-Cha's tail to winnow behind him like a peacock's. In rain, however, he loses all majesty. The plumes hang off his bones in wet clumps and cowlicks. She picks through it with a comb. She often spends the night when she cat-sits—her mother does not mind. She likes to watch TV programs in the evening, like *Wife Swap*, or televised ballroom dance competitions on PBS. In the day, her mother collects basalt stones. She stalks the river and lifts stones from the stream bed to sell to local spas.

Outside, the rain still falls, and inside, the burnt-cream walls surround the girl like a milk carton. Cha-Cha fans across her lap, his throat on her wrist until he stretches and pins her jeans to her kneecap. She rakes the comb down his spine. His hair dries and lifts. A car passes and parts the water on the pavement with its tires.

Then she hears footfalls. Shoes on the flagstones, the porch. A key in the door, though Ms. Feliz won't return for another week. Whoever's out there has not tried the right key. The teeth grind in the cylinder as the person tugs the key free. They try another. The brass rattles against the doorplate. The person swears. They try a third key.

The girl sits very still. She wills the cat to stay with her, but Cha-Cha mews and leaps to the carpet. The girl scans the room for weapons of self-defence. She finds few. She arms herself with a decorative copper bowl.

"Hey, let me in," shouts the man on the porch. His shoes sound light. If she is not mistaken, he's wearing leather soles.

"Hey, Miranda."

The man thumps the panel of glass that frames the door.

"Miranda, I'm locked out."

The girl does not know a Miranda. She rises to her feet and squints through the peephole. The intruder leans with his arm against the glass, a shamrock hat on his head. He looks like he is trying to push the house over.

"Miranda!" he calls again, and aims his gaze straight at her. She recognizes him then. Goosebumps flower over her back. She clears her throat.

"This isn't your house, Mr. Bradley."

She unlatches the door and opens it. The rain has soaked his hat. A vein of water rolls down his neck from the brim.

"Miranda?"

He steps onto the welcome mat and braces his hand on the door frame.

"You're drunk," she says.

This hasn't happened since New Year's, when Colin and Leslie Hall stumbled home to the Singhs' and tried to make an omelette.

"I'll get my umbrella, Mr. Bradley."

The thick tabs of his eyelids sink and flash open. He regards her with suspicion, as if she might be a dream, or a house gnome. He wrings his hat between his fists. Water spills down his thigh. She steps into her rubber boots.

"It's you," he says.

She pinches his coat sleeve and leads him down the flagstones.

"What's the difference between an Irish wedding and an Irish funeral?"

"I don't know."

"There's one less drunk."

She looks both ways and guides him across the street.

"Oh, here's one," he says. "Say 'Irish wristwatch' five times fast."

"Try your key here, Mr. Bradley."

He doesn't move. She steers his hand toward his pocket.

"Say it," he says.

"Irish wristwatch."

"Faster."

"Good night, Mr. Bradley. Happy St. Patrick's Day."

In the troposphere, the clouds drop sacs of water too heavy for the sky. They streak to earth and fill the storm drains, flower-pots, blue plastic pools. The rain spills down the runnel of the road, the pavement worn by all-season tires, roller blades, the cloven hoofs of mule deer. The water searches for hold in ground softer than cement, in the mossy ditches, and farther, the woods, in hot sinks of soil where thousands of eyeless creatures rise to sip at the roots of trees. Here, the Copper River dunks the cow parsnip over their heads, and takes the skunk cabbages too. The birch trunks wade in to their shins.

In the morning, the girl wakes to the tick of Ms. Bradley's heels down the flagstones. Rain drums the roof, fills the window boxes; the trailing geraniums haven't got a hope in hell. Ms. Bradley's car barks to life. The windshield wipers hum on. The girl hears them from her pillow.

On the other side of the wall, across the driveway, over the cedar shrubs, her mother stands in their kitchen and boils water for coffee. She toasts a crumpet in her convection oven. She pours orange juice into last night's brandy snifter. She swirls the liquid and warms the glass between her palms. She will be glad when Ms. Feliz returns, so her daughter will watch *Wife Swap* with her again, or televised ballroom dance competitions on PBS. Her sister married last year, and she and her daughter wore matching mint dresses. She imagines that they will wear these dresses as they watch ballroom dance. They will say words like *floorcraft* and know the difference between a rumba and a bolero.

Last week, she collected twenty kilograms of stones and emptied them into her bathtub. They will remain there until the rain stops, when she will lay them on a towel to sun-dry. Perhaps it's best her daughter lives next door, where she may use the shower. For herself, she rinses her armpits with a cloth. She sprays body mist. Now and then, she showers at the gym. Every night she visits the gym, she sees Miranda Bradley on the cross-trainer in bone-pinching Lycra. Miranda Bradley squeezing ninety pounds on the abductor-adductor machine. Miranda Bradley hinged by her hip blades in full locust pose over a Swiss ball. When Miranda Bradley enters the change room at the same time as her, the girl's mother waits for a private stall.

Now she sips brandy-laced orange juice and plunges the coffee grinds and butters her crumpet. Twenty paces east, in Ms. Feliz's guest bedroom, the girl tucks her sheets under her mattress. Cha-Cha sits on the windowsill and strikes the glass with his paw. The girl answers in English. She says, "I am making the bed just now. Hold your horses." The cat spots an eye of dust on the floor and curls his shoulders. His tail swipes back and forth against the frame. The girl joins him at the window. Four raccoons file from the cedar shrubs. They march tallest to smallest, their eyes flashing like coins from their blindfolds, their bellies wiping the grass. The girl fetches the boiled eggs from the fridge and greets the raccoons outside. She has never seen a raccoon in the daytime. Perhaps their hovel flooded. Or do they sleep in trees? The girl knocks an egg against the porch step and peels the shell. She cups the soft moon in her palm and stretches her arm.

Across the street, Mr. Bradley stands so close to the window his breath mists the glass, and he must clear two holes for his eyes. Also, he wears his wife's housecoat. He can't wear his own anymore, because last week he got food poisoning from Papa Dum's. The terry cloth still smells tangy to him, of gastric acid and ghee. He does not tell his wife he borrows her housecoat. He is unsure why, but over the week it turned into an item to conceal.

From the sitting room, he can hear their Barista Express pressurize two thimbles of espresso; he has not learned yet how to adjust the settings to one thimble. The news plays behind him on TV. The murmur keeps him company, like a café. Though this morning he listens for a reason. Colin from 1216 heard rumour of a planned dike breach. They want to divert the river from the next suburb, which is larger, he said. It is unclear to Mr. Bradley if the subdivision is larger, or the residents' incomes, but he needs to know when to start sandbagging. Worst-case scenario, he owns an inflatable air mattress. He heard that in New Orleans, people floated on anything they could: bookshelves, nightstands. An air mattress should do better than that. They're engineered to float.

Across the road, the girl from 1213 approaches a troupe of raccoons. He worries the beasts will nip her fingers, or contaminate her hand with fecal matter. He watched a program on raccoon roundworms last week. The parasites can cause human blindness. The girl crouches in Esther Feliz's yard and reaches her hand to them. Rain stretches the tank top down her ribs.

The girl has not brushed her hair yet. Raindrops trickle down her part and harden the knots into clumps of steel wool. The bushiest raccoon traipses toward her. She plants an egg for him in the grass. He dips the egg in a lawn puddle and lifts it to his mouth. The other raccoons sniff toward her too. Rain has slicked their pelts into spikes around their necks. She deposits another egg. Across the road, the shadows shift in Mr. Bradley's window. He's wearing a bathrobe, she realizes. The cloth is lilac. His breath fogs the top pane except two finger-width gaps for his eyes. For the first time, she feels outnumbered. And cold. Her nightshirt's so wet she must hold up the armholes. She tips the eggs onto the lawn and retreats inside.

In the ripe, photosynthetic bathroom, she shucks her clothes over the shower rod. She stands blue and naked in the mirror and rubs her shoulders with Ms. Feliz's lotion. In the mirror cupboard, she finds six vials of oil. She selects primrose and wipes it over each wing of her collarbone.

Ms. Feliz's tortoiseshell housecoat hangs on the door. She slips inside it and leaves the bathroom, the hem trailing her heels. She would like to phone her mother, so Mom will microwave her a cup of chocolate and sit on the loveseat to parse her hair. But the longer she waits, the sweeter the nausea she feels behind her belly button. She felt a similar sickness after Mom recycled her diorama of a Kwakiutl longhouse. In return, the girl assaulted her *National Geographics* with a hole puncher. She knelt with a stack from 1994 to 1998 and opened everyone's pupils. Her mother cried, then forgave her. The girl felt terrible. But as she punched holes into Jane Goodall's eyes, into the eyes of race camels and a grey reef shark, she sensed for the first time her imprint on the world. Today she does not sense her imprint but the thrill of endurance. She folds her homesickness into one chamber of her heart and tastes it when she chooses, like a salt lick. She stands in the living room now and faces away from her mother's window, toward the Bradleys' house. Mr. Bradley kneels on his carpet and kisses a giant, black-shelled crab. An air mattress, she realizes. She watches from behind her curtain. Her cheek fills with salt.

Twenty paces west, the girl's mother rinses the grit from her river stones. She separates them by size—thigh stones, facial stones, molar-sized stones for the toes. When her daughter returns, she will book them both a massage. They will lie side by side, which they have not done since last summer. Therapists will map stones up their spines, the same stones she lifted from the river. They will plant stones behind their knees and sink them into their foot arches. She does not remember when her daughter became the only person she thinks about. She knows her shoe size, her jean size. She knows which shops in the mall fit small, and that her daughter will not wear a pencil skirt because she thinks her ribs are boxy. The girl's mother prefers this shopping to her own, which she has not done in a while. She selects boughs of teen dresses from the racks and the clerk folds them in tissue. She thinks about dinner as she kneels before her bathtub and washes stones. On the first night her daughter slept away, she still cooked her meal. She arranged green beans on the plates with rice and breasts of Shake'n Bake chicken. She tented the plates with foil and knocked on her daughter's door. They dined at Ms. Feliz's table, which looked the same as her table, except the salt and pepper shakers were shaped like teeth. But her daughter said she wanted to cook for herself next time. She called it an exercise in independence, which she will present to her CAPP class. The girl's mother still cooks for two, because it feels silly to measure one serving of rice, or sixty grams of linguine. Now she has half a pizza in her fridge, one bowl of angel hair pasta, and one-half of a trout. She has never liked leftovers. They make her feel old.

Twenty paces east, the girl sits in Ms. Feliz's window and watches Mr. Bradley step onto his front porch. He has changed from the bathrobe into cream slacks and a cashmere sweater. He carries a box in his hands. When he jogs off the porch, he ducks under it to avoid the rain. He crosses the road and knocks on her door. She knows he has seen her—she's sitting in a window. You can't ignore someone if you're sitting in the window. He rings the doorbell. She tightens the sash around her waist and answers it.

"You're home," he says.

"Hi, Mr. Bradley."

The rain has notched blemishes into his cashmere sweater. They look to her like a colony of ticks.

"I wanted to apologize if I scared you last night."

"It's okay."

"I brought you chocolates."

He presents a Saran-wrapped box, the plastic beaded with the same wet ticks as his shoulders.

"It's green. For St. Patrick's Day."

The cardboard is black, not green, but the chocolates are filled with peppermint, so perhaps that's what he means.

"Can I come in?"

"Here?"

"I'm soaked."

He removes his shoes and follows her inside. She sets the chocolates on the mantelpiece. By the time she turns, he has already sat down on the loveseat. She does not wish to sit beside him. On the only armchair, Cha-Cha sleeps in an immovable crescent.

"Would you like a glass of lemon water?" she asks.

"Sure thing."

She fetches the jar from the kitchen and pours two glasses. The wheels of lemon do not pass the shoulders of the jar, but she wants one. Before she has time to consider, she plunges her hand in. She clasps a lemon slice and squeezes it like a fish. After she's done it, she's not sure what she was thinking. She lifts the lemon to her mouth and sucks its pale triangles.

Her gums shrink. She wipes her hands on her housecoat and carries the glasses to the living room.

"Merci beaucoup," says Mr. Bradley, in terrible French. He pronounces the *p* as in chicken coop.

"De rien," she replies automatically.

"They still make you take French class?"

"Yes."

She lowers herself onto the edge of Cha-Cha's armchair.

"That's good. The French know how to do basic tasks very well. Like toast," he says. "And kissing."

She tries not to look at his sock. He has crossed his leg so the foot floats at his knee. The argyle drips off his toes and smells of overripe bananas.

"Learn anything good today?" he asks.

"It's Saturday."

"Oh, yeah."

"Does your wife work Saturdays?"

He looks surprised at the mention of her.

"Yes. How'd you know?"

"I'm perceptive I guess."

One kilometre upriver, before the mayor can issue sandbags and order a planned dike breach to minimize damage to the surrounding communities, and indeed as the mayor's public relations manager, Mindy, books a helicopter to ferry him to the site of the breach so that he can explain the benefits of a controlled dike release to the media and members of the concerned public, and as the mayor himself stands at the

Tim Hortons in town with his executive assistant, Marcelle, to select donuts from the pastry counter because he's a city official who arrives at a controlled dike release with a box of crullers for his staff and crew, and back in Copper Waters, as the girl's mother tires of waiting for the sun and dries stones with a hand towel, then fills the pockets of her Barbour coat so she can show her daughter next door—she always shows her daughter first; she thinks of it as a blessing—and as the girl sits in the living room with Mr. Bradley and wills the phone to ring, or for her mother to knock on the door, or anyone, even Mormons, even the Census, and as Mr. Bradley stands and says, "Want to see something cool? Be right back," and jogs across the street for the air mattress, as he opens his door, one kilometre upriver, the water in the soil loosens a tree's roots from the dike—not the one they intended to release, but another dike, smaller, closer to the Copper Waters subdivision, and as the tree collapses, its root system tears a score of soil from the levee and water bursts through, charts a new channel toward the subdivision at the rate of five hundred cubic feet per second, or enough to fill an Olympic-sized swimming pool every three minutes. Mr. Bradley steps back onto his porch with his velveteen air mattress. The plastic is heavy; it forces him to stoop. He almost does not see the mud water heave from the creek. A sinewy rush of it, the brown of upchucked peanuts, overtaking the sidewalk ginkgo trees and Colin Hall's Chevrolet Camaro. The girl watches Mr. Bradley from her living room window. She turns when he does. The water rages down the street—eight houses up, then seven, then six. Twenty paces west, her mother stands in her living room, pockets filled with stones. The water crashes over the cedar shrubs and shudders against her windows. She cannot see out. The water seeps under the door.

The girl collects Cha-Cha in the belly of her housecoat and climbs the stairs to higher ground. On the first floor, water already laps at the heels of the dining chairs, the sides of the couch. She watches the flood from Ms. Feliz's bedroom window, which sits opposite her mother's bedroom window. She shouts for her mother, but her voice is licked away by rain and the surge of water. Outside, the river has bowled Mr. Bradley off his feet, but he clutches the air mattress and drags it under his chest, so that he shoots downriver with the stolen debris—a yellow kid slide, a backyard barbecue, and four corpulent raccoons that paddle beside him in a row. The girl can reach the roof from the attic, which is not really an attic but a series of questionable floorboards and raw insulation. She considers staying in here, to keep out of the rain, but the air smells of itch and sawdust. The roof hangs low enough to open the hatch. She sets Cha-Cha down and hoists herself up. She stands on Ms. Feliz's roof and searches for her mother on their own roof. Or the Singhs two houses down. Or the Halls. But she sees no one. The rain rolls down her neck. Inside, fatty brown water laps at the first stair. It fills the bathroom. The wisteria sucks at it; the hyacinths stand straighter. The peonies open their petals and sing.

Ship's Log

An accounting of the voyage of:

HMCS *RUPERT*

(Led by Captain Oscar Finch and Navigating Officer Clementine Finch a.k.a. Nan)

Sailed: Monday, April 17, 1919

From: Sudbury, Ont.

Bound for: The Orient

TUESDAY, APRIL 18

1600

Light breeze from west. Temperature warm. Clear skies except one cloud the exact shape of the birthmark on my thigh, which looks like a bicycle wheel with spokes.

I'm knee-deep in a hole to China. Progress has slowed since my Nan's noon inspection—must shovel for width now, as well as depth. "China's a long drop," she said. "We'll want room to stretch our limbs."

1630
Went in for a glass of milk at quarter past the hour and Madame Dubois from No. 12 parked her Flivver over my hole. Progress further slowed. She's brought fruitcake and belated regrets re: Granddad.

Weather as above.

1633
I think Dubois's Flivver is a Jabberwocky. (See *Through the Looking-Glass and What Alice Found There,* page 28—"The Jabberwock with eyes of flame came whiffling through the tulgey wood and burbled as it came.")

1640
Dubois's fixing a pot of tea. Visit will be longer than hoped. Tried crawling underneath Jabberwock. Shovel wouldn't fit.

1650
In China, people walk upside down. That's why they wear those limpet-shell hats. The wide brims prevent the Chinese from falling out of the sky.

1654
In China, the sea is made from tea. During the third century, the drink was so prized that the provinces boasted their wealth through tri-annual tea festivals where every member of every town paraded to the beach with masks and fireworks and dragon kites and offered their leaves to the waves in a celebrated public sacrifice. That's why each

coast tastes different. Most of the South China Sea (near Hong Kong) tastes like jasmine, but the Gulf of Tonkin is rosehip, and the Bay of Bengal, chai. The East China Sea is primarily green (there are a few local variations), and the tides of the Yellow Sea ebb/flow peppermint. The Formosa Strait produces a particularly strong brew of ginger root because Taiwan prevents open-ocean dilution, says my Nan. The Chinese don't drink their sea water, though. It's too strongly steeped.

1700

Madame Du*bore* still here. She asked me why I haven't kept the roses hydrated—the ones on the dining room table, from the parish memorial. "Un petty dry," she called them.

2100

Temperature: warm. Wind: not there. Sky: the colour of Granddad's toe after he sailed home from Panama last May to fight the German alphabet boats, which he never did in the end because they wanted him in the Pacific aboard an "armed merchantman," which is stupid because ships aren't men and they don't have arms and we're fighting the Germans not the Chinamen so why send my Granddad to Hong Kong?

Nan cut me a slice of fruitcake for dinner. She'd misplaced her own appetite again. John Cabot did not discover North America on fruitcake. I found a block of semi-sweet chocolate in the cupboard and ate that instead.

I miss Nan's old cooking. We haven't much in the cupboards now. Oats, farina, dried apricots, molasses, chestnut paste. We should arrive in Hong Kong within the week if I maintain shovel speed. (I reckon I average a foot an hour.)

I used to read with Granddad before bed. We're more than halfway through *The Narrative of Arthur Gordon Pym of Nantucket*, and the *Jane Guy* has just been captured by natives, but I won't finish without him. Maybe tomorrow I'll aim for two feet.

WEDNESDAY, APRIL 19

0715

Pleasant Mermaidian breeze from east. Some clouds.

Wanted to dig another foot before Nan got up. Found her in the living room on the arm of Granddad's button-back chair. She was leaning forward and her shadow made a falcon on the secretary and the fishbowl that sits on top of the secretary. The ribbon of her nightgown was untied and it dangled in the fishbowl, but I don't think she noticed. When she moved, it glided across the surface like a Jesus bug.

I saw her breast. It was shaped like a triangle and hung over the pokey parts of her ribs. Then I noticed the slice of fruitcake in her lap and the cashew clenched between her index finger and thumb and the dried cherry floating above the fishbowl gravel. I asked if she slept. "With the fishes," she said. She laughed and her bones made a stepladder in her chest. I took the plate from her lap and said I'd feed Aquinas later.

I made porridge like Granddad. I simmered the oats in milk and vanilla until the oats plumpened and milk clung to each grain like melted wax. Nan declined a bowl. I left her with the swordtail.

1300

Dead calm. Sky like when Granddad made blueberry sherbet for the parish picnic on Dominion Day.

At the pit's deepest I've dug to my thigh. Starboard side needs work. My shovel's caused three casual worms, but I think they'll grow back. The soil's firmer now, less like cookie crumbs and more like dough. Nan says it's clay. In China they bloom bowls and teacups instead of tulips and that's why we call it chinaware. There's broken pottery everywhere and in Szechuan province the lawns are mosaics. I'll bet Chinamen cobble shoes with ultra-thick soles.

My own oxfords are soiled with mud. Nan hasn't noticed. She's in the front, milking the crocuses.

1420

Found a live floater abreast the keel! He wears a scarlet tunic and bearskin hat—potential deserter from the Royal Guard? I conducted a proper interrogation, but he said very little. (He appears to be made of tin, so I suspect his jaw is quite stiff.) I don't think he's a threat as he is little bigger than the palm of my hand—he will stay aboard as boatswain and I shall watch his behaviour. I went inside to introduce him to my navigating officer and found her in the bathroom applying white paint to her face, an emptied box of cornstarch on the toilet seat. Conversation as follows: "Nan?" "Captain Oscar." "What are you doing?" "Putting on my face." The plaster terrified her eyebrow stubs into fossils, and when she smiled, her forehead cracked. "But you already had a face." Her hand rose from the sink, which was filled with white gook, and she slapped her cheek. "Without makeup, I'd stand out in Hong Kong like a polka-dot thumb." Her palm smeared circles and stretched loose flesh to her nose, to her eye, to her ear. She reached behind her head and her cheek drooped to the corner of her mouth. She didn't have enough hair to hold a bun and her fingers left sponge stamps on her scalp. I asked what I ought to wear and she suggested Granddad's uniform, and I thought Granddad sailed for Hong Kong in his uniform, but apparently that was the British one and he has a Canadian one too, but they look almost identical. I went upstairs and found the uniform on Nan's bed. It's large, but I reckon the waistband will hold if I wrap the belt around twice. The pants are funny. The bottom of each leg is wider than the thigh. The shirt's got a large collar and a blue-and-white-striped kerchief, which I don't know how to tie because I was only in Boy Scouts for a year and Nan secured the knot at the beginning and I never untied it. My favourite's the cap. The tally reads "HMCS *Rainbow*," which is a silly name for a ship so I'll probably cross it out and write *Rupert*. Nan's got a navy photograph of Granddad on the dresser. I'm a spit image.

I'm hungry, but the weather's fouling, so I should return to deck. Winds blow fresh and there are dark clouds on the eastern horizon.

1800

In China, there's a pyramid of mandarin oranges on every corner. Because there are so many orchards, everyone helps themselves, and the farmers replenish the pyramids every morning.

In China, they have dens where sages and scarlet women and gamblers and poets puff on the stems of poppies like pipes. Then they have extraordinary dreams, like none that you could ever imagine, and sometimes the dreams tell the future.

1830

Tried to make porridge for dinner, but the milk wouldn't pour from the pitcher. Gave it a slosh and tried again. One drop dripped out the mouth and down the side of the jug. Lifted the lid and found a golden bulb lodged in the spout and six more golden bulbs floating in yellowish liquid. Fished one out for inspection. Its skin felt like a waterlogged chicken thigh, with a hundred spots where the feathers might have been. I squeezed and milk gushed through my fist, trickled down my sleeve into the crease of my elbow. Called for Nan. "Apricots," she said. "I'm necromancing the apricots."

Made porridge with water.

1900

Nan's face is papier mâché and the whites of her eyes look yellow like she's been soaking apricots there too.

I think she's been in my room. I found a pile of white shavings on my pillowcase.

2030
Monsoon! Brisk gale, downpour of rain. I worry my pit will cave.

2040
Tried standing over pit with umbrella. Proved terrifically dull. Went back inside.

2045
There is a slice of fruitcake on a plate in the fishbowl.

2300
Tried to play Chicken Foot with Nan, but she preferred to spell words with the line of play. Had to find Granddad's Double 18 set so that she'd have enough tiles. He bought them on his first sail to Bombay in 1892. They're ivory with ebony inset pips.

Nan's poems:
"Tick tick tick tick"
"Cherry tart, crispy heart."

My poems:
"Tongues clicking, licking"
"Mango meat. Yum."

This game would be easier if the tiles had letters instead of dots.

THURSDAY, APRIL 20

0800

Rains have ceased, clouds clearing. Light airs, temperature like dishwater. Pit walls have maintained structure, but there are two inches of mud at the bottom. Will commence drainage after breakfast.

0830

Breakfast: one-quarter jar molasses plus two necromanced apricots.

Painted a molasses moustache above my lip, and Nan said I made a very fetching George V.

Told her the hull flooded two inches and she said that was the size of my mother's tumour. I don't remember my mother well, but Granddad said she was a dish, which means pretty.

1100

The boatswain and I drained the pit and dug another half foot. We're hip-deep stern to bow. It's harder to shovel, which means we're getting close. (We could be digging through a cement road in Hong Kong and we wouldn't even know.) Crew's complaining of thirst. Maybe the navigating officer will have lemonade inside.

1105
Nan's not in the house. The dining table roses are face down in the vase. Stems spike from the glass at 180 degrees and the water magnifies the heads into clown noses.

1109
She's not in the yard either.

1400
Scoured the coast. Found Nan in Mr. Arden's wood, picking flowers from the riverbank. (Fortunately we've had a dry spring and this stretch of the stream is dry.) She says his April day lilies are the finest in all of Ontario. We gathered four baskets, then lay between the stones in the riverbed and watched an eagle collect grass. Nan tried to string the lilies together stem by stem, but her rings kept sliding off her fingers and we could never remember where the *clinkity-clink* clinked from and they're coloured the same as the pebbles. So I did most of the stringing and my chain grew to two fathoms long. We wound it through her hair over her shoulder across her collar around her waist up her arm. She looked like the Faerie Queene of Edmund Spenser. I had to memorize from Canto XI last year for school. "Be bold, be bold, and everywhere, be bold."

1800
Light airs, some clouds, temperature cool.

I've promoted my boatswain to quartermaster. After writing my last entry, we dug for four hours. The pit's to my shoulders now, and if I bend my knees slightly, it's as deep as my chin.

My shovel ripped a hole in Granddad's trousers. Nan wasn't mad. She helped me trim the pant legs to above my knees and now I trip less and my shovel speed has increased by at least a couple of inches. We were sailing south at almost a foot and a half an hour, but we're inside now because I feel like someone is shovelling the inside of my stomach. In China they believe in karma, which is like Galatians 6:7—"whatsoever a man soweth, that shall he also reap"—and I wonder if I feel like this because I cut those worms in half.

Chinamen also believe in reincarnation. After death you come back to earth as something else. I hope I don't come back as a worm.

I hear shouting.

1804
Dubore's driven her Flivver into my pit.

I hath slain the Jabberwock.
(O frabjous day! Callooh! Callay!)

1900
We had to stick Dubore's floor mat under the wheel and push from the front grate while Nan cranked the ignition, and I fell in the mud twice.

She found Nan's appearance "startling" and threatened to call a nurse the moment she arrived at a telephone.

She wanted to take me home with her, so I hid inside Granddad's chest, which is where I am now but with the lid open a crack so I can see.

The air in here itches.

1910

In China there are fields of garlic and rows of ginger and rivers of soy sauce and hills of peppercorns and plateaus of cumin and mountains of five-spice and clouds of star anise. And the grass is made from lemons.

Someone's on the stairs.

1920

Nan's got rid of Dubois. And she knows for certain that she does not own a telephone and does not like driving at night so she probably won't come again until morning, which gives us till then to get to Hong Kong.

2030

Dug to my nose. Pressed my ear to the ground, and cross my heart I heard wind chimes. We're a few fathoms away at most. Soon I'll be able to crack through to the other side, but I hear Chinese cement is extra strong. (It has to hold more feet because did you know there are a lot of people in the Orient?) Was extra careful around worms, but it's hard on account of the dark. Nan called me in—said we were close, real close, and that we should enjoy our last evening in Sudbury. She wants me to help her look smart for our arrival.

(Her flower chain has fallen off, but the individual lilies are mostly unharmed.) I have to pack too, but Nan says we won't need to bring much. My stomach sounds like Madame Dubois's Flivver. Might try to make semolina pudding from the farina in the cupboard.

2055
My pudding's erupted.

Details later.

2110
Left the farina and milk on the stove while I braided flowers into Nan's hair. This took longer than it should have because A. I don't know how to braid, B. a clump of hair fell out her skull each time I ran the comb through, which was C. gross, and D. hard to hide, but E. I had to hide it because Nan used to have hair down to the bottom of her spine, black as the ink in this fountain pen.

I maybe put in F. too much farina or G. too much milk, and now H. it's vomiting.

Scraped what I could from the pot. It tastes like sand.

2230
We've boarded the ship, but Nan doesn't want me to continue digging just yet. I write by the light of our last candle because we are saving the lamp oil for navigation. I packed: my good breeches, a clean sweater, matches, Granddad's Double 18 domino set, his pocket watch, *The Narrative of Arthur Gordon*

Pym of Nantucket, chestnut paste, this log, an extra pen. Nan's packed nothing, but she's dressed grand—silk tea gown plus the fox and mink furs that Granddad gave her after they got married and Granddad's mother's pearls. She's wearing both furs at the same time because she says it's "bloody Siberian" out here, which means cold. I collected the flowers that fell off her chain, into two baskets this time, and I'm going to try and fix a few to her hat.

I don't think it's how Chinese girls dress, but she says she feels like Queen Mary so I guess that's good?

We're going to play dominoes.

2345
Light airs. Temperature cool, clammish. Skies blacker than the bruise on my right knee, which I think I got from unmooring the Jabberwock. Didn't realize it was this bad until I started using my legs as a writing desk.

Nan and I engineered a domino track, which winds over the whole deck, portside behind Nan's rear, then overtop the tin of chestnut paste to the bow, where it figure-eights around my rucksack and me, then starboard to the stern, over *The Narrative of Arthur Gordon Pym of Nantucket* and under the handle of one of the overturned baskets. We tried to make it climb the ship wall, but the tiles wouldn't stay vertical.

Nan wants me to pinch her cheeks to add colour because harlots wear rouge and ladies get proper blood flowing.

But she's still wearing cornstarch.

FRIDAY, APRIL 21

0015

I don't like pinching Nan. Her skin feels like butterfly wings. She dozed off so I stopped.

I guess I'll dig when she wakes.

0018

The air out here must be even blacker than my bruise.

0020

Nighttime sounds like this: *hiss, chortle, shwoo-shwoo, crackle-crack-crackle-clickle*.

The first three I attribute to the wind.

I've sent my quartermaster in a dinghy to investigate the last.

0021

Can foxes eat sea captains?

0022

I want to go inside, but Nan's asleep.

Maybe she'll wake up if I light the lamp. We'll sleep in the house and I'll just get up extra early to finish digging.

0030
No luck. She's out cold. I even tried coughing very loud. I'm out cold too. But awake.

Our domino track looks like the Great Wall of China.

Maybe it will defend our empire and keep out the enemies and we'll be safe as long as we stay within the tiles.

I just won't move, that's all. I just won't move.

0035
In China the girls bathe in milk and sleep in silk and walk in threes under parasols through gardens. The women wear chopsticks in their hair and fold the future into cookies. The men are warriors, calligraphers, alchemists. They make dragons from paper, fireflies from powder.

0040
I miss Granddad.

0045
I forgot the tin opener for the chestnut paste.

Maybe if I read *Pym* aloud he'll hear me.

0515
I fell asleep under Nan's mink. My neck hurts and I feel like I spent the night in an oyster shell. Sun's below the horizon, but I can see without the lamp. Hair's wet from dew or oyster

spit. It's cold. I'm a bloody Siberian. There's very little wind. Dead calm.

Real ships can't sail without wind, but this isn't a real ship with real sails so it doesn't even matter. It's a hole—a stupid, stupid, stupid, dirty hole.

Nan won't answer me. I didn't want to be rude and shake her so I made loud awake sounds instead—banged rocks on the chestnut tin, etc., but she's a heavy sleeper.

I want to go inside.

I'm scared my toes are blue.

I want to go inside.

0520
I wish he was here. I wish my Granddad was here. I wish he was here. I wish he was here I wish he was here I wish he was here I wish he was here I wish he was here I wish he was here I wish he was here I wish he was here I wish he was here I wish he was here I wish he was here I wish he was here I wish he—

I hear burbling.

A whiffling in the tulgey wood.

Shook Nan, no reply.

It's coming.
The frumious Bandersnatch.
The Jubjub bird.

The jaws that bite, the claws that catch me if I leave this hole, so I am hiding under Nan's fox. She's—

My toe, my stupid-stupid-maybe-frozen-blue toe just knocked over the Great Wall of China.

She's not answering.

I wish he was here I wish he was here I wish he was here I wish he was here I wish he was here I wish

My Sister Sang

Seated and stowed.
Thank you, all set.
[sound like cockpit door closing]
Oh, that fucking door again.
What's wrong?
This.
Oh.
You have to slam it pretty hard.
[sound like cockpit door closing]

This one is: PLANE DITCHED IN COLUMBIA RIVER AFTER MULTIPLE BIRD STRIKES. Three serious injuries. One fatality. Forty-three passengers treated for hypothermia. On my desk Monday morning: the stats, the snaps, the autopsy, the tapes. (The FLAC files—we still say tapes.) Linguists identify speech—loss of thrust, loss of trust, one five zero knots, one five zero, not. I take the acoustics. Engine noise, aircraft chimes, whether the captain has reclined his seat.

~

Flaps one, please.
Flaps one.
What a view of the Columbia today.
Yeah.
After-takeoff checklist.
After-takeoff checklist complete.
[sound of chime]
Birds.
Whoa.
[sound of thump]
Oh shit.
Oh yeah.
Uh-oh.

~

Sometimes you hear the pilots snap photos: Would you look at those Rockies. Or photo of the FO clicking a photo of that fighter.

Also, they swap jokes: Welcome to the George Herbert Walker Bush Intergalactical Airport.

[sound of laugh]

I can't fly anymore. Free flights, if I wanted, but I can't coax myself past security. I take trains.

Mayday mayday mayday mayday.
Caution, terrain terrain terrain.
Too low. Terrain.
Pull up. Terrain.
We're goin' in the river.
Say again, Jet Blue?
Pull up. Pull up. Pull up. Pull up. Pull up.

The *Oregonian* featured the accident front page. I bought a copy at lunch. The girl's on A3: BACKUP SINGER DIES IN PLANE CRASH. In the photo, she's surrounded by honeycomb. Her hair's the same colour. Yellow in the wax light, how sun warms through a sheet of gold tack.

Case #1734512
Name: VERNON, Joy
Age: 19
Race: white
Sex: female
Cause of death: cerebral hypoxia
due to: asphyxiation
due to: aspiration of water into the air passages
Manner of death: drowning

In the autopsy photo, her eyes are open. Brown irises. Eyes like wood like warm like walnut. Report says sclerae clear. Report says ears pierced once each lobe and nose unremarkable.

She sang backup for Fiona Apple, says the newspaper. And LuAnn de Lesseps. She also released a single of her own, which you can purchase on iTunes for $1.29.

My sister sang before she married. Christian pop, which her manager sold as gospel. We weren't religious. Our car had a Darwin fish. But her manager said there was a market. He said, "Praise radio will eat her up with double ketchup and a side of fries."

I never liked him. He wore T-shirts with milk stained down the front. "Cheerios," he'd say. "Sometimes it's so hard to get them in the mouth."

The new linguist started today. She'll analyze the resonant frequencies of vocal tracts. "F-values," she calls them. How we form words from the lips and the teeth and the tongue and the lungs. She combs her hair very smooth. I think she must use a bun setter.

I brought a coffee to her computer station to introduce myself. I said, "Well, if it doesn't work out here, I think the CIA is hiring."

She typed the rest of her sentence, then pointed to the small ceramic pig on her desk. It had a Post-it note. The Post-it said *Cunning Linguist Jokes $1.*

She's bright. But she knows she's bright, which makes it less attractive. Still.

~

We work in the basement, where you don't see the sun. You see: two computer monitors with equalizer waves; desks made from highly recyclable aluminum; ergonomic chairs, whirly. Our lab is fragrance free and climate controlled, volume controlled, light controlled. Plants cannot grow here. We keep a synthetic lemon tree by the vending machine.

~

To isolate the voices on a CVR tape, you have to clear the extraneous noise in layers. The engine roar, the static. Like filing sand off a fossil, stratum by stratum. Blowing off the dust. Audio archaeology, let's say. Let's say Indiana Jones.

I like to listen to routine takeoffs and landings. The pilots sound like performance poets. I picture them crinkled over the control board in black berets, anemic fingers snapping, clasping espressos, eyes cast to the far corner, too cool for contact, for the stewardess with the pretzels and the can of V8.

Flaps five.
Flaps five.
Flaps one.
Flaps one.
Flaps up.
Say what?
Flaps up.
Flaps up.

~

My sister toured once, ten years ago, after her junior year of high school. She hit the major towns on the praise radio circuit. Lubbock, Texas, to Lynchburg, Virginia. "Lynchburg," I had said when she showed me her itinerary. "Lynchburg?"

She shrugged. "They have the world's largest evangelical university."

The tour was eight weeks, to private Christian schools and rodeos. Her merch team sold chastity rings. She brought me home a mug that said TEAM JESUS and filled it with prayer jellybeans. Red for the blood you shed. Black for my sinful heart. Yellow for the Heaven above, and so on. I still have them. I think she meant it as a joke.

She died in childbirth. A C-section that led to a blood clot that led to a stroke. We talked on the phone the night before. She told me they had painted the nursery yellow, which the decorator described as String. She said that yellow can be shrill; it's hard to get yellow right. She said she got it right. She said, "You know the colour of a wheel of lemon when you hold it to the sun?" I said, "Perfect. Have you settled on a name?" She said, "Yes. Jaime. Because on paper it reads like *j'aime.*"

Jaime turned four last month. I talked to her on Skype. When she grins, she thrusts her chin at you like a goat. I can picture her in a garden this way, neck craned to the sun, like day lilies and sunflowers. Heliotropism, I think it's called.

After lunch, I found Joy Vernon's single on YouTube. The song is called "Delilah," the video shot at her father's bee farm. She sings against a barn wall in a breezy shirt dress, and she picks her banjo. A low, pinging banjo, against that wall, and her voice is blue and dusky.

Halfway through the video, I felt a brush at my elbow, and I turned to find April the new linguist behind me in her chair. She had wheeled it from her desk across the aisle. I shifted, and she rolled nearer.

"She's lovely, isn't she?" she said when the video ended.

"Yes," I said.

"Could you play the song again?"

I dragged back the Play bar. We watched the video from the start. Bees in the wisteria. Joy's hair in her eyes as she bows to see the strings.

"Carrot slice?" said April. She had packed her lunch in a bento box. Everything compartmentalized. A slot for the chopsticks.

"Thank you." She passed a carrot into my palm. It looked carefully cut. On a diagonal, the edge serrated.

"I used to work in homicides," she said. "Voice ID from emergency phone calls, and so on." We still faced the computer screen—Joy at the barn again, strumming the banjo between verses. "This one case, the vic was an opera singer." She paused to snap her lunch box. "I never liked opera. But after a week on the case, I ordered her recording of *Evita* online. I listened to the tracks over and over."

I nodded. The YouTube video had ended. April turned to me. Her cheeks looked worn somehow, smooth and unsunned, but as if the skin was pulled too tightly to her ears.

She continued, "When you replay a voice in evidence for eight hours a day, you can almost know the person. And when you catch a glimpse of their life before, you get immersed. I get immersed. In the knowing of them."

I stared at her.

She looked down. "Maybe that's unprofessional."

When she raised her eyes, I was still staring. She held the eye contact. In that moment, I understood that she understood that I understood everything she said.

I often see her at the vending machine. She never buys anything, but she slides her eyes over each item through the glass. I stopped once. When she noticed me, she turned toward the elevator. I said, "Too many choices?" and she smiled and waggled her lunch kit.

You get into the habit of transcription: sound of Smarties dispensed from the machine, sound of Coke can, sound of leather soles on a vinyl floor. Sometimes you try to adjust the levels. At the crosswalk, when I race a yellow light. Sound of honk. At home, when the neighbours yell and one of them unhooks the fire extinguisher. Sometimes my fingers stretch for the mouse.

After work today, I returned to the newspaper stand and bought the last fifteen copies of the *Oregonian*. I don't know why. But they were only a dollar each.

For Jaime's fourth birthday, I mailed an Easy-Bake Oven. She loved it. The cookie dough turns pink. She said to me on Skype, "This present is my number two favourite." But I want to send a gift I didn't find on page one of the Toys "R" Us flyer. Origami, maybe. Her mother loved origami. I have this Polaroid of her folding paper swans—thirty of them—for her classmates on Valentine's Day instead of cards or cinnamon hearts. Are four-year-olds into paper?

My sister and I bought ants on television once. *An entire colony, queen included.* We converted our fish tank into a two-storey formicarium—poured plaster over a plastic wall, over the clay tunnels we had shaped with our palms. Plus leaves and sand. The leaves you call "forage," plant material for grazing livestock, a term we adopted. Livestock. Can't play soccer after school—have to check the herd.

She sang for them. I played rhythm: chopsticks on an empty plastic jug. The ants go marching one by one, hurrah, hurrah. Work songs. You could watch them for hours, and sometimes we did. The entire colony shimmering through the chambers, a still black line, though every ant moved. Frames of celluloid projected on a screen, like a river, like blood cells. How motion can be static—it gets you thinking.

When we spotted an ant too close to the cheesecloth, she would fetch petroleum jelly from the bathroom, and we fingered streaks of it around the lip of the aquarium. I told her they harvested Vaseline from jellyfish.

She said, "Do not."

I said, "Do too," and smeared a daub of it into her bangs.

We later experimented with radio and production speed. Which is to say, crawling. Which is to say, with speakers situated on either side of the formicarium, do ants file faster to the "Imperial March" or ABBA? The study proved inconclusive.

After a couple of months, the plaster moulded and ants found their way into the kitchen, into the paper sack of flour and the dried figs. My mother made me dump the tank in the park "at least two blocks from our house." My sister started piano. She signed up for voice lessons twice a week with an

Italian woman who sang off-Broadway. I took up coin collection. There was money in coins. Ha, ha.

~

And they all go marching down.
    To the ground.
        To get out of the rain.

~

A quick hello from your cockpit crew. This is Flight 166 with service to New York. We'll be flying at thirty-eight thousand feet, mostly smooth, for four hours and fifteen minutes, takeoff to landing.

~

I've heard the cabin safety announcement so often I could probably be a flight attendant. In preparation for departure, please be certain your seat back is straightened and your tray table stowed. There are a total of eight exits on this aircraft: two door exits at the front of the aircraft, four window exits over the wings, and two door exits at the rear of the aircraft. To start the flow of oxygen, reach up and pull the mask toward you. Place the mask over your nose and mouth. Place the elastic band over your head. The plastic bag will not inflate.

~

I have this shirt with a soundboard printed on the front. The caption says "I know what all these buttons do." I think a pilot could wear this shirt also.

~

Today April wears a wool sweater the colour of eggshells, the colour of string. She's hennaed her hair very red. Poppy, I'd say. I think she must attract hummingbirds.

At break I stopped behind her at the vending machine and watched her scan the items. I don't even think she brought her wallet. I stood there for a full minute before I caught her staring at me through the glass.

She turned. "Go ahead. I'm not in line."

"Me neither," I said.

She shifted her eyes to the potted plant.

"You know they're scented?" I said.

"I'm sorry?"

"The lemons."

She drew her eyes to the yellow baubles of plastic fruit.

"Real wood too," I continued. "We voted for it last year. They emailed options from a catalogue."

The elevator dinged open and one of the techs from the fifth floor strolled out behind us. April stepped for the door. I stepped with her.

"What were the other options?" she said.

"Orange." I walked inside the elevator and leaned against the far wall. "Banana. Bamboo."

"I would have voted bamboo."

The elevator opened at the main floor. I followed her

through the lobby into the courtyard, an urban "green space" designed with white-slab cement, birch mulch, a stand of honey locusts, and a fountain.

I said, "They described the lemon trees as *evergreen*."

She said, "Well, I don't suppose they lose leaves."

We bought coffees from an espresso bar across the street and carried them back to the fountain—a rectangular pond like a wading pool, with a hunk of granite in the centre for the spout. In fact, I'd seen the fountain used as a wading pool a few times. And as a bird bath. And as a urinal. But such is public art.

I offered her a piece of my croissant—one stuffed with chocolate, so what I said was *"Pain au chocolat?"*

She said, "No, thank you."

I sipped my coffee.

She said, "I'm not supposed to have this, but you want to hear?" She outstretched her iPhone, the white wires of earbuds looped around her thumb.

I nodded.

"One of the survivors posted it on YouTube."

She offered me an earbud and plugged the second into her own ear. We bowed over the phone. I could feel the friction of the space between our foreheads. There's a point where technology mimics the past. iPads like slates, like the Flintstones, like chisels. The phone felt divinatory—as though we should be bent over a bowl of water.

She tapped the screen and opened the video. She pressed Play.

Rain blew into the camera, diagonal sheets of it into the aluminum and brown water. The camera jolted up and you could see people, their orange life vests, crowded onto the wing. The rear slides had extended. They floated uselessly, like slapstick rubber chickens. What you could hear was shouting. Passengers shouting to passengers in the water—*Grab here, grab my hand.* Passengers shouting to passengers to swim away—*Dive, before it goes.* Crew shouting to passengers to stop shouting. What you could hear was rain. Drumming into metal, into hard water, pinging off the life vests. And a continuous chime from the interior of the aircraft, *ding ding ding,* like your door's open, a friendly reminder before you leave the parking lot. And there, in the corner of the frame, you could see her treading water. She had floated the farthest from the wreck, her hair starfished out around her shoulders. She drifted farther from the plane with every paddle. Her mouth opened and closed, but not in communication, her eyes unfocused, or focused on a distance. She was singing. You could see she was singing.

~

To fold a paper swan, your paper must be square. With sixteen newspapers and scissors from Reception, you can cut a lot of squares. I began with a lifestyles story on the 2002 Miss America. I pressed her face in half. Then I folded the same line onto the reverse side, white space for an AT&T ad. I followed a dotted diagram online and ignored all the video how-to's. I don't like to have to pause and rewind.

April found me at eight thirty, after she cycled back to work for her phone. I had moved to the floor at this point, to the strips of paper I snipped from the squares. I stored the completed swans in an emptied recycling box—fired them from where I sat, like paper planes. Paper swans. Nose first into the box, or onto the surrounding carpet.

When she saw me, she backed up, then stepped forward, then stood very still. "We used newspaper for my guinea pig," she said. "You look like my guinea pig."

"You have a guinea pig?"

"I left my phone."

"Okay."

"When I was twelve." She folded her arms over her ribs. "Her name was Rosa."

She helped me fold swans. We plugged in her iPhone. We listened to "Don't Cry for Me, Argentina" on repeat. By midnight, we needed to borrow another recycling box from the lab across the hall. I noticed we both folded A3 so that Joy Vernon's face pointed outward, from the tail of the swan, or the wings.

I think I can fit the swans into three oversized boxes from UPS. I'll mail the Polaroid of my sister with the first parcel. In the photo, she hovers a blue gingham swan above her head. She balances the wings between her fingers like she might let go. Like she knows the swan will stay suspended when she drops her hands.

Worried Woman's Guide

They removed Bea's ovaries during that week in June where you can't walk a foot without killing a caterpillar. A week after the oophorectomy and she was rolling up her driveway in a chair rented from the Princeton hospital, her ex-husband's son, Huck, at the helm. He pushed the chair over inside-out caterpillars, and when he bisected one with a wheel, it curled at both ends. She had expected it to slice right through. Sun soaked through the turmeric-dyed cotton of her caftan and made her thighs look jaundiced, until the shade of a cottonwood tree up the drive reblanched her skin and backlit the bumps that puckered from her hair follicles. She tugged the hem over her knees. When she let go, the cloth shrugged up her thighs and flashed the white of her new briefs. She adjusted her hem, crushed the cotton into her knee, and hoped to Jove that her ex-husband's son failed to catch a glimpse from his eagle-eyed view at the handlebars.

She had awakened that morning to find her morphine button missing and a bronze stilts walker of a man hovering at the door, his neck bent to fit the frame like that giraffe from the Santa Barbara Zoo with a ninety-degree spine.

"Beatrice Cooper?" he said. He wore a snap-button shirt with a rattlesnake stitched above the breast pocket, and he hugged a felt hat under his armpit, his biceps squashing the crown into his ribs, so that she thought it might pop inside out.

"Bea," she said.

"I'm Huck." He stepped through the frame and straightened his neck. "Parker's son." He had a hook nose and eyes like a cat. When she stared at him, he blinked a lot.

"How old are you?"

"Twenty-four."

She had never met him as a boy, though they had sent one or two photographs on Christmas cards. The divorce had been amicable enough for that.

"The hospital still had my dad as the second contact." He dropped his eyes to his boots. "You know he moved to the coast ten years ago."

"I know."

Huck didn't reply right away. Bea could hear the wheels of a stretcher squeak past her door.

"Well, I work in Kelowna now," he said after a few moments. "So he phoned me."

"Where's my sister? Louise should have been called first."

Huck withdrew the hat from his armpit and ironed his palm around the puggaree to re-inflate the crown.

"Your nephew broke his arm," he said. "Something to do with a tether ball pole." He laid the hat on his head and hitched his thumbs under his belt. "I'm to stay with you for a few days until she comes. Dad hired me to do some work."

"Work?"

"Some landscaping."

"Landscaping."

"Some landscaping work."

The morphine, turns out, gets cut on day seven. But not without a consolation bag of incontinence briefs, the *Worried Woman's Guide to a Happy Hysterectomy*, and a supersized bottle of codeine-coated acetaminophen. The nurse also suggested a panty girdle for post-operation support, but that wasn't included.

Huck roved the wheelchair across the lawn to the sunroom steps. During the summer of their second year of marriage, she and Parker painted the cottage walls robin's egg blue. Two tracts of granite wall cut through the centre of the lawn on either side of a footpath—the only relic of a stone cottage planned by coastal developers before they lost funding. Parker had promised to clear the walls to build a pond, but Bea liked the haphazardry. She lined them with seashells from the coast and pretty, dead things like dragonflies and snakeskins, and four springs ago she planted a honeysuckle vine to climb one of the sides.

Huck strolled from behind with her knapsack over his shoulder. His eyes darted between her and the stairs until he bent his knees and heaved the chair into the air. Bea yelped and lurched forward. He lowered her back to the grass. He stood there again.

"Can you make the steps?" he asked.

"Yes," she said. She pressed the hem of her caftan over her knees again, before she leaned for the stair banister. She found the ground with her sandals and heaved herself up. Huck guided her elbow. Something spasmed in her groin and she froze with a sandal on the first stair. She snatched her arm from Huck and pressed it against her chest as she lifted the other foot. He waited beside her as she attempted the next step.

"Keys are in the zipper pocket," she said.

He shifted the sack so it straddled his chest, grabbed the keys from the pocket, and unlocked the door. Bea reached the top step and waddled into the room, pelvis first and bowlegged.

"Can I offer you a glass of iced tea?" she asked him.

He moved forward as if to beat her to the fridge, then paused and sank onto the loveseat. "That would be fine, ma'am, thank you."

"You'll call me 'Bea,'" she said from the next room. "'Ma'am' ages a gal worse than cigarettes."

They sipped iced tea and commented on the artichoke. Nine feet wide and six tall—biggest he'd seen outside of Castroville, Huck said. Then he complimented the tea—did she make it from scratch? She said she had better things to do, and how was his mother? His mother was living on the coast now and very fine. Yes, a nice house; no, without a pool (who needs one a block away from the Pacific). Sandy (not Sadie) was male and almost finished high school. He planned to become a veterinarian.

"You have kids?" he asked.

"Well, I hope they'd be here instead of you if I did."

"You want any?"

"They didn't tell you the nature of my operation, did they?"

He shifted in his chair.

"Did you ever want any?"

The rainbow plastic strips of the seat sweated under her thighs.

"At one point maybe," she said.

Parker had volunteered in the maternity ward during his final year of med school, and Bea used to drop him off. Most mornings she had nowhere to be, so she would walk him to the delivery room doors, kiss him brassily, then meander back through the corridors. She often paused at the nursery. The pastel bundles wriggled in their beds and the nurses fed them or changed diapers, their motions always so swift with practised duty.

Bea arched her spine to stretch a crick in her neck and the flesh of her shoulders squeaked against the back of the sun chair.

"I'm going to roast Louise like a root vegetable," she said. She inhaled the warm plastic air. "So. What is it you do when you're not landscaping?"

He clasped the brim of his hat between his finger and thumb and rotated it left across his brow. "I band hummingbirds."

With her vision blurred the sunflowers on the drapes melted with those in the garden, except she didn't have sunflowers in her garden so they just melted. She uncrossed her eyes.

The drapes were hideous, but they added colour to the vegetables she could see through the window. She mostly planted vegetables, because if you can't eat the produce, why get your hands dirty, except to add colour, but then, why hang drapes? She might plant sunflowers and retire the curtain, but tall crops made her feel short, and at forty-eight she was only getting shorter.

The surgeon had kick-started her menopause, the final milestone, and now all she could do was wait. Wait for her spine to sickle, her breasts to droop, until it was time to remove those too. It ran in the family. Her future would be breastless and bloodless—pre-pubescent, post-woman. That seemed to be how the chips fell.

The artichokes should have been picked days ago. Jumbo globes the colour of lizard bellies bobbed off the stalks like street lamps, the bracts open on those directly facing the sun. The flesh would be stringier than floss if she didn't pick them by tomorrow. Time passes like molasses when you're bedridden. She used to hang a flower box out her window, but after a couple weeks the daffodils succumbed to her I'll-let-it-rain philosophy. Now her sill was bare save a line of nine avocado pits. To plant an avocado tree, she always said, but really she delighted in their smoothness. A perfect sphere to cup in your palms as a child might her largest marble. In the sun they'd all shrivelled too.

She fell asleep after the iced tea and stayed asleep minus two hobbles to the bathroom. She'd been awake now for an hour and twenty-three minutes and felt okay—pain subdued thanks to the codeine-coated acetaminophen, of which she'd taken three. Maybe a little weak on her feet, head in the clouds, but from her bed the sky looked cloudless, so where did that leave her head? She wanted to get the shears. She could hear Huck in the kitchen, landscaping what smelled like buttermilk pancakes. She climbed out of bed and swallowed a fourth painkiller. Then she tiptoed or floated to the garden shed.

Now the artichokes loomed above Bea on the ends of their sceptres, two flies humming and bumming around the highest globe. She stood half-hunched beside the plant, its jagged silver-green leaves clawing at her sleeve, at the aquamarine garden loppers in her hand. She angled the loppers at a low-flying artichoke, about level with her nose, and squeezed the handles, but when the blades nipped together, they only pushed the stem away. She grasped the stalk with a fist and pressed the handles together with her hip and other hand. The globe plunked to the grass between her pigeon-toed feet and she nudged it with her heel. It rolled into the dirt bed and stopped short of a mound. Ants streamed back and forth between the mound's peak and the edge of the grass, and when they reached the choke, they forked into two threads. Anthill removal was another project she and Parker never got around to.

On the taller stalks the artichokes were just beyond arm's reach. These were the globes nearest the sun, their scales glutted with yellow light and beginning to yawn. She stabbed the loppers into the lawn, leaned on the handles, and stared at the house. Huck stared back from her bedroom window. She drew her shoulder blades together and raised her chin—embarrassed that she felt embarrassed for getting caught outside. The sky was overcast now. Clouds trapped the heat and the warmth hung boggy and thick around her limbs. She needed a footstool. She leaned more weight into the handles and the point sank deeper in the grass. Huck continued to watch her like he didn't realize she was staring right back. The shadow from the eaves darkened half his face as his hat might have done, but she fancied she could still make out the green of his eyes. She stepped onto the path, leaving the loppers vertical in the lawn, and padded her feet along the gravel.

~

In an ant colony, sterile wingless females form the proletariat—hired as soldiers or workers depending on the size of their heads. You know you've found an anthill if the ground is alive, the dirt sifting beneath your feet. You lie beside them. The ants with oversized heads explore your hips. More follow. They swarm your legs, your feet black with their exoskeletons. You wear ants for pants, thousands of hooks stamping your skin.

Expect to itch, the nurse said. Before this, you had not shaved since your first year of marriage. Must pick up moisturizer. Must reread chapter three of the *Worried Woman's Guide to a Happy Hysterectomy*, "On Shaving."

~

She couldn't scratch her crotch because now Huck was below her, spotting. One of his palms shined out, fingers stretched and ready should she tumble from her two-foot footstool.

His other hand held his hat, flipped upside down to collect the artichokes. Bea clutched a lopper handle in each of her hands. She arched back and looked sideways at the remaining fruits, sun piercing through the clouds now and blotting out the stems so the globes looked suspended from fishing line like a mobile of the solar system. Around the stool the grass was studded by the chokes decapitated before Huck volunteered his hat. She pressed the fulcrum of the blades against the stalk and clipped. The artichoke plopped to the grass. Bea stepped down and Huck, who thought she was falling, palmed her butt. Her feet stayed pegged to the stool—she wondered if he could feel the extra padding.

He whipped his hand into his jeans pocket. With eyes pinned to the grass he bobbed his chin to the empty nectar feeder that hung from the eaves.

"That won't attract hummers without red," he said.

The feeder was a wedding gift, another unused relic. She looked away from it and told him she'd like to go to town.

Her cottage dwelt in a pocket of wood between Keremeos and Cathedral Park—a fire access route away from the turquoise bridge, which led to the Ashnola Forest Service Road, which led to the Similkameen River and Highway 3. Keremeos was home to fifty fruit stands and Hedgehog Central. So local vendors sold hedgehogs and peaches, but no panty girdles. The next nearest Canadian town was Osoyoos, and it was almost faster to shop at the General Store in Nighthawk, Washington, but Nighthawk was also unlikely to sell panty girdles. Bea shifted in the passenger's seat to transfer weight off her groin. She spread her thighs and cracked the joints in her hip sockets. Her knee grazed Huck's hand, which rested on the clutch and did not flinch at her contact. She drew her knees back together and grazed his hand a second time, then threw her stare at the windshield, which was slicked with the butterscotch entrails of flying highway insects.

"So you band hummingbirds," said Bea.

He raised his chin in a way that indicated he heard.

"Why?" she asked.

"Identification."

"Why?"

"To learn."

She pressed her lips together and glanced at the rear-view mirror before she could again ask why. Her eyelids were thicker than average and made her look like an insomniac or a poet or French, but with her lips sucked in she looked like the speak-no-evil monkey, so she puckered them out. To plump her lower lip she rolled it toward her chin until the luminous inner lining glimmered in the mirror—then she drew it back. She rotated her head to aim the perfected pout at Huck and realized he was already looking at her, so she darted her eyes forward and opened the glove compartment. Inside there were road maps, balled-up receipts, and a sleek aluminum case. She drew the case onto her lap and unclasped the buckles. The interior was lined with velvet, and a hole in the centre cradled a digital scale. Shape-appropriate slots carried a magnifying glass and surgical tweezers. She pinched the glass from its slot and examined her fingernails, then the stick shift and the hairs on Huck's knuckle, then his eye, which bulged in the lens and startled her. She tucked the magnifying glass back in its slot, buckled the case, and slid it into the glove compartment. "You ever call yourselves bandits?" she said.

"What?"

"Hummingbird bandits."

He didn't reply. Out the window the topography softened more and more into grasslands, badlands. Hills of canvas rolled on either side of the highway and clumps of thistle prickled from the hills. When she drove Parker to the interior thirty years ago, he could not take his eyes off the tumbleweeds. He said he felt like Clint Eastwood and didn't seem to notice that after five minutes the desert dwindled back into orchard. Sure as rain, grapes replaced the next kilometre of sand—rows of vines sea-nymph green and plump with irrigated water.

"Do you date?" said Huck.

"What?"

She pressed the fabric of her dress into the nooks of her armpits as the truck passed the sign for Osoyoos.

"My boss in Kelowna is around your age. Needs a lady to spend money on."

Around her age.

"I can give you his number."

She searched her mind for a sly response, but could not form the words in her mouth before the moment stretched too long.

Find your belly button. Now slide two fingers down—one left, the other right, until each rests halfway to your hip bones. These are your ovaries. Your estrogen epicentres. The estrogen softens you, shapes sex traits like wide hips and breasts. Between your wide hips you can draw a constellation. Start from the ovaries. Trace your fingers in toward your pubic bone. These are your fallopian tubes and the horns of Aries, first sign of the zodiac, the ram. The face of Aries is your uterus. The surgeon left the uterus, but your horns are removed. They've uncuckolded your ram.

She chose the scarlet panty girdle with Bettie Page on the package because the other ones were labelled like tofu—firm, extra firm. It cinched belly button to thighs and she almost bought the matching garter. When they returned to the cottage, Bea lit the stove and put on a pot of water the size of a small bathtub. She added rock salt and lemon juice and, when she couldn't see through the steam, six artichokes. More than she and Huck could eat if the artichokes weren't the main course. Boiling artichokes was like boiling crabs, except she didn't imagine their screams until she made the comparison, at which point she did. Then she imagined the human heart as a thistle that had to be boiled and peeled and dipped into butter, and felt silly so she left Huck to mind the stove. After a few minutes he set the pot on the table over two oven mitts, and brought the saucepan of butter and an enamel bowl for their scraps. The panty girdle made Bea sit up straighter, which made her cross her legs at her ankles, which tightened her hips and piqued the pressure on her groin. She peeled the first artichoke bract gingerly, but there isn't a polite way to suck off the flesh. The scales piled in the scrap bowl and she and Huck watched each other from behind their green goblets, gums grinning like thirsty kings.

"How do you catch a hummingbird?" asked Bea. She had been planning this question since the drive, letting herself imagine a dream catcher, webbed with twine and turquoise beads and down feathers.

"A mesh net."

"And then what?"

"We measure them. We weigh them."

"Isn't that like weighing a helium balloon?"

"We wrap the bird in a nylon sock."

"A sock?"

"A nylon knee sock."

Bea scraped her bottom teeth against the meat of an artichoke petal. The butter was forming crystals in the pan.

"Tomorrow I'll clear those rocks," Huck said, and wiped his thumbs on the tablecloth.

"It might rain," she said. Her palms hung off her wrists, fingers glossy with butter. "I won't have you work in the rain."

After dinner Bea's skin boiled, so she stood in her panty girdle and sports bra, the lights out except the bulbs around her vanity. She traced a red splotch that bloomed across her chest in the shape of Australia, then slid out the door to the full-length mirror in the hall. She could hear boot steps. On the bottom stair, up one, two, and pause. A dull pain swelled between her thighs, and when she clenched them, it didn't help. The boot steps resumed and Bea kneaded her toes into the rug. She leaned her shoulder against the wall and waited for a shadow to spill onto the top stair. A shadow did spill onto the top stair, then up the wall, followed by Huck in his cowboy hat.

He turned away immediately. "I'm sorry, ma'am," he said, and removed his hat.

She wiped her collarbone with the back of her hand, then wiped her hand on the wallpaper as he beetled back down the stairs. "You'll call me 'Bea,'" she said.

To suck honey from honeysuckle, find a vine and pluck a flower. Tug out one of the stigmas. Insert the bell of it between your teeth and the tip of your tongue. You and your husband used to take turns. He would pluck a stigma and slide it between your teeth, your chin tilted up like a baby bird's. You would scrape out the honey, then slide a stigma between his teeth, and he would re-open his jaw and trap your fingers.

Bea stood before the vine that climbed the granite wall. She cupped a flower between her palms and gazed at the chalice of strands.

"Did you know every day a hummingbird must consume half its weight in sugar?" said a voice.

Huck's silhouette hovered under the eve of the porch. His face was blotted out by dark, but indoor lamplight pooled on the brim of his hat and made it look disembodied. "They need it—some migrate three thousand miles. Honeysuckle's their favourite."

Bea spread her fingers and the flower slipped to the grass.

"I don't mind the rocks," he said, and walked to the other wall.

"Me neither."

"If I take 'em out, that'll be the end of the honeysuckle. Was it you or my father who wanted the pond?"

"Your father."

"Then how about we leave the rocks be."

She smiled and watched him fiddle with the brim of his hat.

"I'm going banding tomorrow," he said. "You can come if you like. I take the pickup, so if it's too much strain, you can rest in the truck."

"Why, Huckleberry, I'd love to," she said.

The trap is made from two rubber rings—the bottom ring a foot below the top and joined by fishing line. A nectar feeder hangs from the mesh roof, and more mesh shrouds the outer circumference, bunched at the top but ready to be dropped on entry of a hummingbird. Huck hung the trap, which he called a "mist net," from a crabapple tree forty-five minutes west of her cottage. They had left the pickup on the highway and followed a brook through the woods until they reached something of a grove. Six crabapple trees clumped in a horseshoe on either side of the stream, their branches deluged with blossoms like over-feathered flamingos, and between the trunks the brook blushed with their reflection. Bea and Huck shared a stump a few feet away.

"And now we wait?" she asked.

"And now we wait."

Bea shifted weight onto her tailbone. The damp air erected the hairs on her forearms, so she unrolled her flannel cuffs and tucked her jeans into her wool socks. "Hot chocolate?" she asked. She had awoken before Huck and had time to get a pot of oats on the stove, as well as some cocoa for the road.

"Sure."

Bea reached for her bag and withdrew the Thermos. A plaid Thermos that she now realized matched her shirt. She unscrewed the lid, and the Thermos mouth released a puff of steam.

"Kahlúa?"

"It's six in the morning."

"Quarter past."

"I'll go without, thanks." He began to wind the mist-net drop cord around his thumb.

Bea poured hot chocolate into a speckled enamel mug and passed it to him, then pulled the Kahlúa from her bag and splashed some into her cup. She added the hot chocolate, clutched the mug with two palms, and watched the mist net. Then, under the theory of a watched pot never boils, she shifted her gaze to the sun, which straddled the horizon and warmed the treetops.

Huck leaned down to tie a loose shoelace and a tag poked from the collar of his sweater, so she stretched forward to tuck it in. Her fingers lingered beneath the wool and warmed against the back of his neck. He flicked his head toward her, the bristles of his cheek scratching her wrist, and she withdrew her hand.

"Do you know the song 'Moon River,'" she asked.

"Hmm?"

Bea clinked her teeth onto the lip of her mug, then swallowed a sip. She hummed the first note to test how brittle her voice sounded. In fact, it sounded okay, so she sang a full line.

Her huckleberry friend knitted his fingers together and placed them in his lap. "My mother used to sing it," he said.

Bea pressed her nose into her mug, then added another shot of Kahlúa.

"Bea," Huck said, voice hushed. He nodded to the net, where a hummingbird buzzed outside the feeder, then he tugged the cord. The mesh veil unrolled from the top hoop and Huck opened his aluminum case. He handed Bea miniature scissors, a sheet of metal foil, and a nail file from a cloth bag. "Cut a band from here and file the edges," he said as he withdrew a Ziploc bag of nylon socks from his pocket.

Bea snipped the tiny indentations on the metal sheet, and studied the band on her thumb. It occupied the space of a few spirals on her thumbprint, and she wondered how she'd know when the edges were smooth. She pinched it between her nails and rubbed each side with the file until Huck glanced at her expectantly.

"Hold on to it," he said, and walked to the trap.

Bea followed. The hummingbird's throat shone a metallic red, and its bill needled into the drinking tube. Huck lifted the mesh and slid his arm through, the sock on his fist like a sock puppet. Then the sock puppet swallowed the hummingbird. He peeled the nylon off his wrist and around the bird and withdrew it from the trap.

"Band," he said. Bea presented the band on her thumb, and Huck rolled the lip of nylon up from the hummingbird's legs.

"Can you hold him?"

"What?"

"Hold him," he said, and passed the pointy warm sock into her palms. He pinched the band from her thumb with a pair of tweezers, then crimped it around the hummingbird's leg. He knelt beside his case and placed the digital scale on the grass. "Set him on the scale."

She sank to her knees and hovered the bird sock over the scale, then released it onto the metal plate, her hands domed over to prevent it from falling. "How do you know he's a he?"

"You examine the primaries," he said, and wrote the bird's weight on a pad of paper. "In males, the sixth primary feather is pointed."

Huck cupped his hands under Bea's and lifted the sock from the scale. He unrolled the nylon further and measured the bird's bill with a ruler. Then he slipped the nylon off altogether. The bird glimmered from his palms and flitted up into the boughs of the crabapple.

There was a message from Louise when they got back—her nephew was out of the hospital, so they could stay with Bea for the remaining days of her recovery. She and Huck waited for her to arrive in the sunroom. They sat hip to hip on the wicker bench, Bea in a lavender sundress, Huck in jeans, glasses of iced tea balanced on their laps.

"What'll you do now?" asked Bea.

Huck tapped his index finger along the rim of the glass. "More landscaping?" he said. He sipped the iced tea, then fingered his breast pocket. "Look, I have something for you."

Bea watched him withdraw a folded paper. He passed it to her—the sheet was the size of a page torn from a pocket book and marked with words in all capital letters.

"The recipe for nectar," he said, then pressed a ribbon into her palm. "And something red."

"Thank you," she said, and wound the ribbon around her thumb.

~

One cup sugar, four cups water. No food colouring. Watch the pot until it boils. Scoop sugar into the centre of a glass bowl, then pour in the water. Stir until the grains have completely melted. Wait for the solution to cool and fetch the footstool from the artichokes. Set the stool on the sunroom porch and step up. Unhook the feeder from the eave and weave the ribbon through the links of the feeder's chain. Red to attract the hummers.

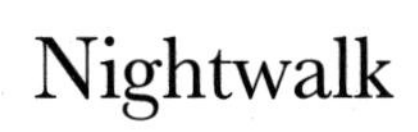
Nightwalk

At Brockton Oval with the painted poles—thunderbird, lightning snake, one over the other like so many mounted heads. A stand of eight totems, cedar wings stretched, wooden goose steppers in a sidewalk sobriety test, place your right heel in front of your left toe, and so on—in clubs they call this the Dooeystep. (DUI-step.) They surround her, the totems, in that malted dark of 2 a.m., 3 a.m., who knows a.m., the digital clock on his dash blinked on and off midnight—always forgetting her watch and her bear spray and her overpriced box of advanced-healing blister cushions. She could stand in the centre of these beams and lift her arms too, lean against one pole for balance, like in theatre trust games: freefall back into carved cedar arms.

Long walk from the causeway in cork-wedge platforms, lily leather T-straps, baby toe red from the cold and the rubbing, and also it has grown toothy. The callus forming what feels like a second nail. Longer walk to the Regent Hotel, where she keeps her toothbrush, Hastings and Main,

Wastings and Pain, the crinkled men and their carts, women rattling inside thin leather.

And now between rains, the warm husk of beach smoke: someone's kept a store of dry wood. It's too dark to see, but she follows the scent. Campfire summers at Sombrio Beach, smooth dusty stones you could build a bed on, the tang of broiled trout and fat apples wrapped in aluminum foil. She follows the seawall, the jogging path, the triplets-in-the-stroller path—smoke crisper as she treks, sharpened by the November wet.

Her dad burned caterpillars in his fifty-five-gallon rusted drum. Great sudsy tents of them, between boughs of the crabapple. Slinky black worms, nested together, fused to one another's curl. How many of them are there? she had asked, and he laughed, tossed his Lucky can into the fire, cracked a second. One million, he said, and that seemed to her the largest number.

Tonight her date lived on Beatty Street, but he drove to North Van, as they do. There's a spot near the bridge, in the firs and the hemlocks, by the shine of the moon, the lights off Grouse Mountain. She said forty-sixty-hundred, and he said sixty. She up-sold him to a hundred. When he dropped her on the causeway, he asked if she had a flashlight. She said no. He didn't either. He said watch out for coyotes, then rolled up his window.

So she strolled on the shoulder, on the painted white line, lane signals above her, the neon arrows and *X*'s. Then a Nissan sped past, backed up, and a kid hucked a spoon. Spoons is a game the suburban boys play, when they're bored of their cul-de-sacs, their *Call of Duty* and *Grand Theft Auto.*

You cruise skid row with a bucket of spoons—plastic from Mickey D's, or metal from Mom's cutlery drawer. Hurl the spoon at a hooker, and if you hit her, you tear off; if you don't, you pull over and climb out for it. A beef-cheeked boy arched from the Nissan, and his spoon skidded in the gravel at her feet. Then the car sped away and his face flapped out the passenger window like a stupid dog's. The spoon was for soup, stainless steel, with a grapevine etched up the handle. It sinks in the pocket of her moth-eaten cashmere like a small stone.

She knows the fire will be Cliff's. Milkman Cliff, they call him, because he sold milk before he joined the navy. He's the only squatter who doesn't sleep in the woods. Colder on the beach, exposed to the wind and the rain and the cops on their horses. But he misses the sea, says why sleep outside without waterfront? He keeps dry—camps in a fort beneath an old spruce. Wears military wool: olive sweater, with reinforced shoulders, cable-knit combat socks. In the daytime he retreats to the trees, or the sidewalks for cash. But he's one of the few who don't use.

The coil of this seawall, how it zigs in and over the bays like a snake, and she could be on the snake's back, stepping over its smooth dry scales. From the beach, the funk of barnacles and kelp and soft-rotted crab. And there on her rock, *Girl in a Wetsuit* in oxidized bronze, sea-green and streaked with seagull shit.

She can see the smoke now, around the next bend or the one after that, a fat black billow of it, like he's burning damp wood. She's talked to Cliff a few times—downtown in front of an RBC bank, or on the water at nights in the park. As kids they both camped on Vancouver Island—she and her mother at Sombrio Beach, Cliff and his uncle in Tofino. She camped in Tofino too, when she was sixteen, and they talked about that. They talked about cold summers and salal berries and crab off the rocks.

She had met him in the park two years ago, in the woods behind Beaver Lake. There had been a show at the Bowl, and sometimes she scored dates in the queues, or at 11 p.m. after the encore. Cheers tapered, then exodus of fans—girls in grunge denim and glow-stick neck hoops, boys without shirts—Converse sneakers and chunk heels in the mud. You couldn't trust college guys—they brought their friends and camera phones and didn't pay. But one boy stood alone in his Thunderbirds sweatshirt. He checked his phone for the time, returned it to his jeans, checked his phone for the time and returned it. She said, Hey. He checked his phone, didn't look up. But when she walked away, he jogged after her. She smoked and he walked with his arms folded over his chest. The night was warm. You could smell the sweet pine and water lilies.

At the lake they sat on a soft mossy tree trunk and talked about unimportant things—You know this park had a polar bear? he said. A polar bear, she repeated. In the zoo. His name was Tuk. She didn't mind the chitchat. Some guys only needed someone to hear them. But then she heard laughter and the ferns swished behind her. Four guys stood between the tree trunks. One said, Dude, what the fuck, and the others kept laughing. A boy with wet lips and greasy eyelids stared at her as he swallowed the last pull of fireball from his mickey. She guessed she had twenty years on him, her cheeks worn for her age, her skin looser. She felt aware of it then. How the skin hung off her biceps. The boy lowered his mickey enough to speak.

Man, I invite you to *my* parties.

He spoke to the boy in the Thunderbirds sweatshirt but kept his eyes trained on her. He still clenched the empty mickey. The bottle ticked back and forth against his chest.

A heavier kid in a Kokanee toque laughed and glanced behind him.

Shit, man, he said.

The Thunderbirds boy wouldn't look at her or his friends. He clutched his phone again and blinked at the screen.

The Kokanee boy tossed his empty in the bush. One of the other guys did the same. But the boy with the mickey held on to his. He shifted the bottle to his other hand. His finger and thumb had been looped around the bottle's neck, and he kept the shape of this ring as he lifted his fist. He stared at it, as though gauging the size. Then he made eye contact with her through the hole. He had an erection, she noticed. He noticed that she noticed and smiled. That's when she called for help.

Dude, said the boy in the Kokanee toque. He elbowed his friend. Dude, look.

Cliff stood on the other side of the clearing with an armload of firewood. He must have been there the entire time. When she met his eyes, he lowered the bundle and removed a bottle from the inner pocket of his anorak. He lifted one branch from the ground and doused it with liquid. She could see green leaves, but when he lit a match, the upper bough whooshed into fire. He strode to them. The guys stared. One said Jesus Christ, and Cliff stopped walking. He stood there in his anorak, damp hair lit by the blaze, and all the boys took off, sprinted into the trees. One stumbled over a fern, cursed as he fisted into the mud, kept running. Her own feet stayed planted. She watched Cliff with his ridiculous torch, and he watched her, until the fuel burned off and the branch loomed skeletal above his head. He mashed it into the dirt, stomped on the embers, then trod back to his pile. She helped him regather the sticks and old bark. He ordered them on the ground by their size—chunks of dead stump on the bottom, a pyramid of slim twigs overtop.

The next week she saw him in front of the bank. She dropped into the A&M market down the block and bought cookies and a carton of milk. She found him again on the sidewalk and plonked the milk at his feet. Hey Milkman Cliff, she said, and his blue eyes lit on her. She sat with him for an hour. They watched the young professionals pass in their young professional leather shoes, ate *Good Time!* strawberry biscuits and swallowed chin-dribbling swigs of the milk.

Her feet slide in her platforms, her hard icy toes, the incandescent red of cold flesh, old flesh. Sometimes after long nights she can feel her blood spider into varicose veins. The smoke from his beach fire looks pearlier now, more acrid, like he's burned old clothes to keep warm. Mouldy socks or plastics from the shore—salty milk jugs, chip foils, smooth blue litter from kids who dig holes and eat Dunkaroos. One more bend in the seawall and she'll see the highest logs in his fort—strange symbiosis between Cliff and the beach kids, the Sunday construction of driftwood houses, which at night he reinforces with old curtain.

She saw his fort only a couple times. One log juts from the bank and props the lighter, card-tower eaves. He'd found the crate of old drapes at St. Vincent's, said it took him all night to tuck the cloth between logs. He lifted each plank, threaded curtain under and over the wood like a pie lattice. You could see wedges of old polyester hydrangeas in the cracks. Swabs of newspaper too, which kept drier than you'd think, the fort shaded by the overhanging spruce. That's how they used to insulate walls, he said. Newspaper. He said in his uncle's cabin he found a newspaper from 1922. He kept the crossword. Folded the page inside his coat next to his navy tag. *The fibre of the gomuti palm*, ten down. *To sink in mud*, nine across. *What we should all be.*

Down the steps to the logs, the beach-side balance beams, slick with rainwater. From the next bend, she can see his fire. And his fort. But his fire is too big—his fort is on fire. Her feet slide again, ankles rolling when she steps to the sand and starts to run. Flames flick over the tilt of his eaves, halo one branch that booms up like a mast. On a log in a row are six empty bottles of nail polish remover. She can smell it now, the acetone, thick and sweetly stinging. The fire is shrinking into smoke—too much damp wood. But flames runnel up and over that branch mast, nip at the spruce bough. She calls Cliff's name and kicks a plank off the centre log. The plank burns her heel. When she kicks off a second strip, the smaller logs fold in, and a swath of curtain. She can see his sleeping bag and wool blanket. The smoke swells into her eyes. She grabs at the bag. The bag is light. She yanks and the canvas shell snaps from the collapsing entrance.

She does not know where Cliff is, but she waits in case he returns for his bedding. She sits on the log with the plastic bottles, the row of them like pellet gun targets. An old *Vancouver Sun* lies ahead in the sand. Inside, maybe the Sunday crossword. *Ring of*, a clue might say. *Pants on, Trial by. Fire escape.* She flexes her palms to the embers, her feet, and warms her toes under a curl of polyester.

She sat with him here last week at the same time. The water was out, and they watched a heron pluck through the shallows, the tide pools lit by the lights off the bridge. Cliff warmed instant coffee in a titanium saucepan and poured hers into a speckle-ware mug. Only got one cup, he had said, waving the pot in the air to cool the metal before he lowered his lips to the rim. They talked again about summers on Vancouver Island, smooth stones, fat apples. He said he and his uncle slept on the beach. His uncle boiled the coffee in the morning with eggshells. Cowboy coffee, Cliff had said. It's good.

At her turn to speak, she told him again how she had visited Tofino when she was sixteen, with her boyfriend's friends and his truck, cheap gin and a case of Labatt Blue. Someone strummed a guitar, she said, "Southern Man," "Pancho and Lefty," and they drank as the tide went out, those stubby glass bottles. You could park on the beach then, she continued. Do you remember? Her boyfriend's Chevy played tapes behind them, his keys still in the ignition. On the last night at low tide, she climbed into his truck and drove toward the ocean. She steered straight at first, past the high-water mark and bars of seaweed. Then at the last moment, she rotated the wheels left and carved donuts in the sand.

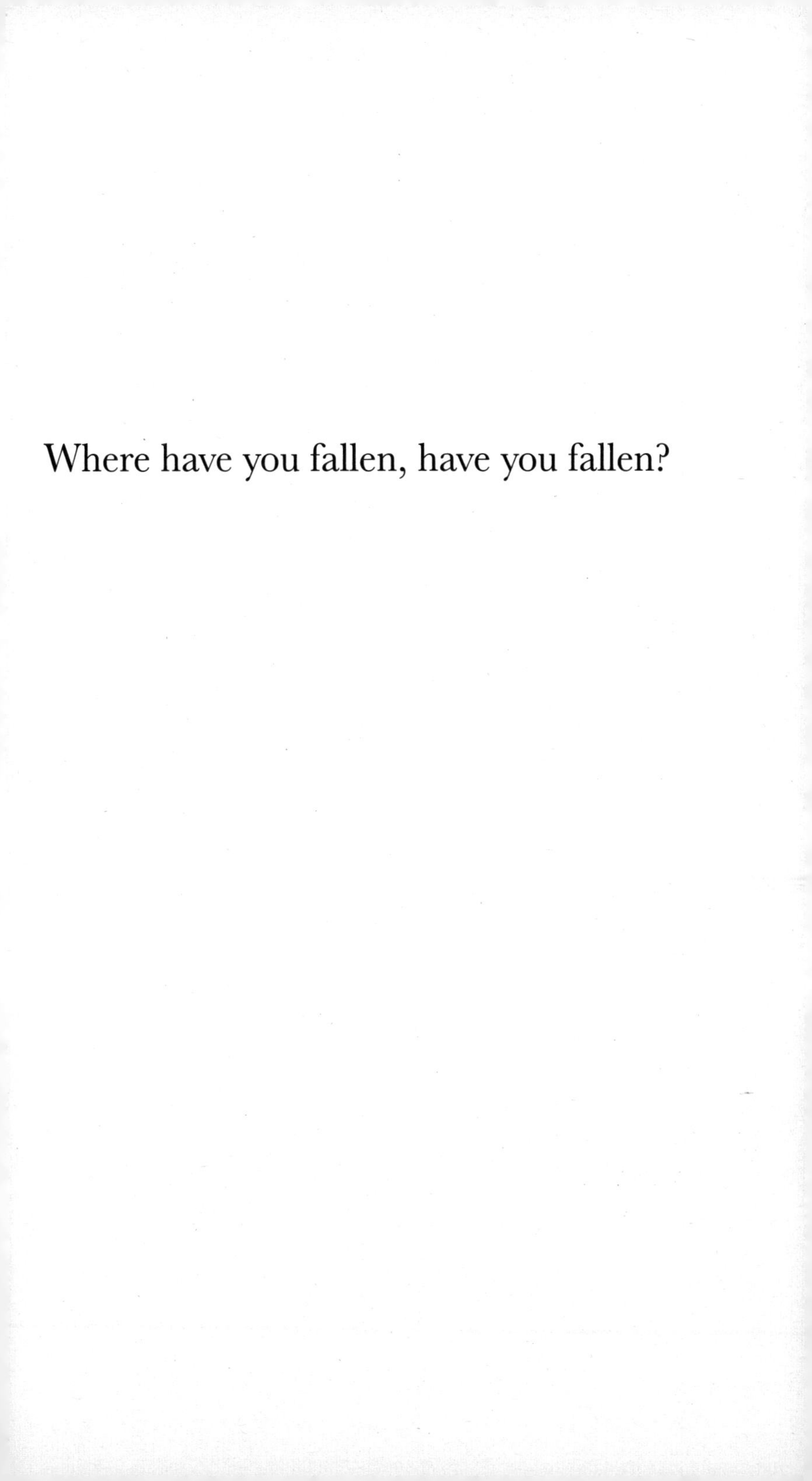
Where have you fallen, have you fallen?

EIGHT

In the long ago, the rivers bore monsters. One dwelt beneath the foam where the Mahatta ran quick from O'Connell Lake, where the river flowed in faces, geometric and flat and reflecting sun like a prism. Every ripple had a mirror, and for every mirror, the monster had an eye. Its tongue lolled beneath the rocks on the shore, and when villagers knelt on the bank to collect water, the muscle would flex, tremble the pebbles, and snatch the villagers into the monster's jaw. When of all the villagers only a young girl and her grandmother remained, Hilatusala the Transformer visited to inquire what had happened. They spoke of their missing neighbours, of the monster with many eyes and its tongue beneath the sand. The Transformer listened, urged the girl to collect water, urged her not to be afraid. So she fetched her pail, kissed her grandmother's cheek, and strode to the river's edge. Before she noticed the shifting gravel, the girl was launched into the air with a speed that knocked her to her back. She opened her eyes to see real birds and clouds and jagged trees instead of their rippling reflections. Then the monster snapped its teeth shut. The fleshy plates that lined its throat shrugged and expanded and slid the girl deeper into darkness, which is when she heard Hilatusala's song. The notes screamed all at once like a raven's shriek and surging water and the whine of a jade knife against cedar. In response, the monster's throat plates shrugged in the opposite direction and the girl was hurtled over its tongue. She landed in the river. Above her, the monster's jowls shook, its lips parted, and the wet bones of the girl's neighbours spewed onto the shore. Spines and sickle ribs and collarbones spilled from the corners of its mouth until the monster had vomited all the villagers and coiled back beneath the surface. And so the girl and her grandmother set to work. They matched ankle bones to kneecaps, hips to ribs, spine to skull, until they reassembled an entire skeleton. Then the Transformer sprinkled the bones with Life Water, and tendons bloomed between ligaments like elastic bands. The muscles grew next, then skin, then smooth black hair, until a villager was reborn. The more friends they reconstructed, the more friends helped them reconstruct. And so it was that notch to groove, vertebra by vertebra, the girl rebuilt her village.

SEVEN

The canoe poked from the pine tree like a wooden wing, and they crouched ten feet beneath it on either side of a stump. Her new friend, Milton, set the plates side by side and sprinkled them with fuel from a plastic lighter. He was the only young person she'd met so far. Everyone else was a friend of her uncle's.

"My grandmother lived up north," he said. "Where they burn food for their ancestors."

Natalie zipped the collar of her track jacket, bounced on the balls of her feet.

"I found this in the *Gazette*," he said. He dug into his pocket and passed her a folded news clipping.

It was the photo all the papers used—her mom and brother at a swim meet. Her brother wore goggles strapped to his forehead, and her mom's good blouse was wet from his arm around her shoulder.

Milton tossed her the matchbook. She struck two matches at the same time and dropped them onto the plates.

"Normally you offer clothes," he continued, as fire ballooned then shrank into smoke. "But the newspaper works."

At the actual funeral in Vancouver, the reverend wore a collar and clerical robe, though he used to say he was a *necktie preacher*, someone who rolled up his shirt sleeves. She couldn't help but notice that his robe looked like a hand-me-down. Faded from washing. Wrinkled at the back where he sat while they played the slide show. She was seated with her uncle in the front row, and could even detect a milk stain on the reverend's chest. It felt so disrespectful, that stain. Here in the woods, under the pine tree, and the canoe kept in the pine tree's boughs, her goodbye felt more sacred. She dangled the newspaper above the embers and let go. Their faces glowed as the paper floated and whirled into the half shell of a sea urchin.

"Do you still have the top?" he asked.

She had found the cedar spinning top yesterday in the surf. It fell from the canoe, she realized later. She tugged it now from her cut-offs and tossed it into the fire.

On the cardboard plates, the salmon shrivelled and curled, the fat spitting in hot pops. Inappropriately, she felt hungry again. As if she had not just feasted.

Milton drew the spool of thread from his pocket and nestled that in the embers too.

"Could you make the fire bigger?" she asked.

"Bigger?"

A smile pricked his cheek, which was otherwise long and flat, unaccented by bone.

"More lighter fluid," she said.

He fumbled with the metal valve and dumped a stream of butane into the embers, snapping the flames vertical. The smoke burned thick from the plates, swelled into her nostrils with the fishy tang of oolichan grease. She watched the flames twist around lumps of camas root, watched the shadows cast on Milton's cheeks, how they flapped across the bridge of his nose like crow feathers.

"Let me tell you about the girl who rebuilt her village from bones," he said.

SIX

All the potlatch guests were in the Big House. They had set the food tables outside, in the covered eating area. The tables were papered now with napkins and cardboard plates. Salmon skins clung from the rims, shrouded the piles of fish bones on the tablecloth. Natalie poured herself pink lemonade as Milton walked to the food warmers and salad bowls at the far end. He uncurled the foil from the salmon plank and lifted a steak with his fingers.

"Come on," he said.

"I'm full."

"It's not for you."

Lemon pulp stung her tongue; she swished her mouth with a swig of someone else's cola and joined him at the table. She'd seen the half porcupines at dinner, the orange meat that hung from their husks in tongues. She hadn't tried one because she had no one to ask what it was.

"A sea egg," Milton told her now, beside her.

She looked up and realized he was watching her. "A what?"

"An urchin."

She took the half sphere and set it on an empty plate. The salmon remained on the cedar plank it was cooked on. Gummy fat oozed between the flesh and silver in spumes, and it slicked the insides of her fingernails when she separated a hunk from the skin.

"Did your brother like camas root?"

She shrugged. He laid a wedge of what looked like sweet potato next to his salmon. "How about bannock?"

"I think we baked that on field trips."

"Where?" He tore a corner from the bread in the cookie tin.

"Squamish." She shovelled wild rice onto her plate with her hand. "A cultural centre."

She liked the feel of food in her palms, the grains of rice squashed beneath her nails with the salmon fat.

"Somewhere between ski lifts?"

"I guess."

She felt embarrassed. Or rather, like she had done something wrong. And now, in this conversation, she was still doing it.

"They taught us to snowshoe," she said.

"Damn. How to top that."

"Ever tried?" she asked, to change the subject. "To snowshoe."

"I can think of one time. With duct tape and my brother's Ping-Pong paddles," he said. "But I think we were trying to ski."

She maintained eye contact as he grinned at her, made a point to not look away first. He dipped his thumb into a jar of pale wax and stepped toward her, presenting his thumb like a birthday candle, like she should blow it out. After a whiff she leaned away. "What is that?"

"Oolichan grease." He jerked his hand as though to smear it on her wrist.

She shrank toward the table and stabbed her own thumb in the jar. Then she faced him and shadowed his hand left and right.

He wiped his fingers on a napkin. "One, two, three, four, I declare a thumb war?"

"Bow, shake, corners, begin."

But after a moment, he seemed to lose interest.

"We should go," he said. "They'll come back soon to clean."

She smeared her thumb in a sunny arc on her plate as he slipped from the wood shelter, into the trees. When she looked back, he was gone. She caught the end of his shadow. It traced the path she found yesterday—toward the cove, the canoe in the pine tree, her friend who slept in its hull.

FIVE

Before the potlatch, Natalie sat next to an Orchid of the Western Sky. The clans were entering the Big House, though some still mingled outside, between the food area and wood clearing. The single flower sprouted behind the stump she had selected to wait out the crowd. Its pouch bobbed under a white hood, between two pea-yellow wings, so the orchid looked like a cheekless milkmaid, all neck and tongue and cotton frill cap, blond pigtails out the sides. It must have been planted. Her uncle said Western Skies were hybrids.

Sage burned on all sides of the clearing—narrow bundles tied with twine and secured in the dirt with rocks. The smoke smelled stiffly sweet and reminded Natalie of the kids at her old school, who shared joints in the snowberry bushes behind the smoke pit.

A man in a sealskin vest stood outside the house. He hacked at a cedar log with his knife, and two young girls with chin-length hair distributed strips of bark to guests. Natalie tied hers around her head as she watched the others do. Then she followed them in.

She selected a bench as far as possible from her uncle, who stood on the other side of the house, his lilac golf shirt tucked into khaki shorts. He was chatting with a local elder and a white woman she figured to be a town council member. His eyes shone pale in the firelight and met her own. When he waved for her to join them, she looked down and pretended not to see.

Someone sat beside her, knocked his knees against hers. She glanced up, saw it was Milton, and turned away.

"I said I was sorry," he said.

For some reason, she thought again of the orchid. Her faceless milkmaid. Its roseate and waxy tongue.

"Christ, you people think *we* hold grudges." He poked her hip. "Well, did you find the wild man of the woods?"

He meant Bakwas. Who fed cockles to the dead and ferried their souls to the other side.

She stayed quiet.

"You look disappointed," he said.

She shrugged. "I'd have eaten his cockles in a heartbeat."

"Don't be silly," he said. "You wouldn't have a heartbeat."

The sound of shaking stones, or beads, rattled from the corner of the house, followed by drumbeats. A man entered from the far edge of the circle. He wore a mask with a black beak as long as the girl's canoe, harnessed to his chest for support. Its lips were painted red, its eyes skyward ovoids, and cedar bark hung in shreds over his back. He cocked the mask left right left right, then yanked a string that snapped the beak closed.

"That's the Man-Eating Raven," said Milton.

The raven capered to his feet, then squatted, then capered again toward the fire, black button blanket flapping at his ankles like heavy wings. Another dancer entered the circle. The beak on his mask was curled like a tidal wave.

"Crooked Beak of Heaven," said Milton. "Both serve the Cannibal at the North End of the World."

The birds leaped at each other, snapped their beaks with wooden cracks that made Natalie flinch each time. The fire threw their oblong, man-eating shadows onto the faces of the guests.

"Follow me," Milton said.

She felt his rough, moist fingers on her elbow.

FOUR

The canoe in the trees must have been carved for a child, because Natalie couldn't lie lengthwise without her calves slung over the edge. She sat cross-legged instead. Next to the bones, which were folded loosely inside a wool blanket. The bundle was wound taut at the feet, but it had unravelled at the hips, maybe picked apart by gulls. A spiny branch of the pine tree poked between two ribs. Plates of a copper necklace fanned over the skeleton's clavicle. The smallest one dangled in the gap above its breastbone.

The dead grey sides of the dugout were chiselled and grooved. Tree needles filled the bottom. The sky was dark now, and in the moonlight the Chinese beads glittered from the hull like discarded fish eyes. They dribbled from a small, capsized cedar basket and piled in the most tilted side of the canoe with the toys—cedar bark tops, buck antler gambling sticks, which she recognized from the museum, and whalebone dice, dotted with black grease. A woven doll lay under the Popsicle-stick ligaments of the body's hand. Natalie lifted a finger bone to compare the doll's eyes with the one she found that morning on the beach, but at the same moment she heard the twigs snap from the forest floor. Leaves rustled; maybe the wind. She wasn't afraid. She wanted to meet the man who fed you cockle shells, who paddled you to the other side, and now she had a companion for the sail. Natalie could return to the girl her second doll, the one with abalone eyes, and they could trade necklaces, her own a silver cross, and the girl could teach her how to spin a top. She never heard of Milton's man of the woods, though she had read up on stories before she came. She read about the thunderbird, who flashes lightning with the whites of his eyes, who eats whales for breakfast. She read about the northern Tlingit boys, who reached the other side by a chain of wood-carved arrows. She read about the Hamatsa, the secret cannibal society who whirl the dances of man-eating birds—the raven of many mouths, the crane whose beak cracks skulls. She wanted to meet all of them. To find that patch of sky where the stars seep light like milky cobwebs, where the indigo between suns is gauzed.

"Natalie," shouted a voice from a few metres down the path. A beam of light tore between the branches of her tree.

Her left thigh felt like it was filled with sand, so she shifted to release it from her weight. The canoe squeaked against the pine bough and a bead rolled off the dugout lip, but she couldn't hear it land.

"Natalie," the voice said again, from directly under her.

"I know you're there. I see the canoe." The flashlight beam smeared the canoe's lip, then spilled back into the branches.

"I'm sorry," he said. "It was a silly trick."

She hugged her wrist around her knees and watched the beam shiver back and forth on the tree trunk.

"I let her go. It was supposed to be funny." Milton's voice paused, silent for her response. "Fine. Stay there all night."

She gathered the spilled beads one by one and dropped them into the basket.

"See you tomorrow at the potlatch?" he said.

She could hear his sigh, and the swish of leaves between his shoes as he shifted.

"It doesn't really hurt them."

THREE

The flowers were shaped like paper crowns, as fluorescent as the sockeye that hung in strips outside the smokehouse. Milton stalked the bush with a ball of twine. He looped knots around the wax heads of neighbouring black-eyed Susans and through the lichen-crusted fingers of an overhanging plum tree.

Natalie watched him work from the grass, which reached her waist when she stood and tented over her as she sat. She could feel the air get wetter as the sun drooped copper and low behind the trees.

"Milton," she said, and fingered the porcelain beads in her pocket. "What's across the ocean?"

His eyebrows lifted and wrinkled his forehead as he stepped away from the tree.

"Is it China?" she asked.

"I don't know." He shrugged. "Maybe. Maybe Japan?"

"Oh." She clenched a bead inside her fist. "Do things wash up? From the other side?"

"Like what?"

"Beads. Chinese beads."

"You found Chinese beads?"

He peeled a slug from his bucket and wrung it between his fists. Slime farted from its tail in wet ribbons, and she stared as he massaged it into the twine.

"Some objects drifted here from old merchant ships," he said. "Maybe beads."

He plucked another slug from the bucket. "Sometimes we traded with the immigrants. The rail workers."

"What about canoes?"

He stared at her. "The canoes are our thing, moron."

"No, I know." She bent low to tie her shoes so he couldn't see her cheeks. "But what if you found a canoe in the forest? In branches."

"Where were you?"

"Nowhere. What if."

He worked his slugs fist by fist along the twine and didn't respond.

She eyed him through the stalks. "What's this for anyhow?"

He smiled and stepped back to review his strings, then leaned against the tree. "You'll see."

She lay back in the grass and shut her eyes.

"Some clans used to bury their dead in trees," he said.

Her eyes opened. She looked at him.

"Or on scaffolds. But trees were easier to come by."

He said this slowly, as if recounting a ghost story. She couldn't tell if he was trying to trick her.

"That way, their souls were nearer to the wild man of the woods," he said, with a small smile.

"Who?"

"Bakwas. He lives with the spirits of the drowned, in an invisible hut in the forest."

Milton paused, his eyes on the bee balm. A hummingbird had whizzed through the strings, and it hovered above the plant, bill needling into the scarlet throat of a flower.

"He feeds them the meat from cockle shells," he said. "Ghost food. Eat it and you become like him. That's how he takes the dead to the other side."

Natalie considered this. Considered whether her mom and brother counted as "spirits of the drowned."

"You buried people in canoes instead of coffins?" she said.

"Sometimes," he said, and removed a spool of white thread from his pocket. "Sometimes cedar boxes."

She shifted her gaze to the hummingbird. Most back home were brown, but this one was silver winged, its tail dusted green, a high-necked collar of iridescent fireweed. The bird dipped under the balm and cornered right for an exit, but a wing caught the yarn. Its feathers were welded to the slug slime.

She stumbled up, cried, "It's stuck," even though its entrapment was plain and Milton didn't seem bothered. He cupped the hummingbird in his palms, then clutched it with only one. His other hand guided a threaded needle into a hole at the base of the bill, then thrust it through. He folded the thread so he could hold the needle and knotted end, then spread the fingers of his other hand, releasing the bird with a gentle bounce. It zipped the length of the thread, then rebounded back, and forward again, whisking the air in hard ovals like the propeller of a beanie, so fast that its shape blurred into an exhale of green wind.

"Do you like it?" he asked. He held the thread like a kite.

She didn't answer. She speed-walked past him, past the plum tree, then sprinted down the overgrown path to the woods.

TWO

"You're the preacher's girl," the older boy said. He wore jeans and a black beater, and he tied his bandana like a pirate.

"He's my uncle."

Natalie lay stomach down on a picnic table. She flicked the cedar bark top she found that morning in the surf. It spun out from her fingers until the nose dipped into a crack between the table planks.

"So you're going to the potlatch tomorrow? They always invite your uncle."

"I think so."

The older boy carried an empty margarine bucket. He squatted between the peonies in the centre of the church flower bed and sifted wood chips through his palms.

"What are you looking for?" She studied the line on his

biceps where the flesh turned darker. That was their goal back home—sunburned summers of FM radio, diet colas, and squeeze bottles of olive oil.

"Slugs."

She laughed. He didn't. She flicked the top again, but it wouldn't go, and the boy leaned forward onto his knees and snatched something from the paddle-shaped shadows of leaves on dirt. A slug—fat and Dijon coloured. He held it out for her, the slimed crest of its back contracting between his fingers.

"What do you do with slugs?" she said, and pulled herself up. She felt the fiddleheads graze her calves from her back pocket, so she lifted her haunches to remove them.

"That's secret." He grinned and dropped the slug. It landed in the margarine container with a *thwack*. "Why'd you move here?"

"Secret."

The boy pinched another slug from the chips. This one was black. A pearly string of slime linked it to the ground. "Show you mine if you tell me yours."

She waved the fiddlehead in figure eights through the air and watched him scour the bed. He paused and straightened his spine, watched her watch him.

"My mom and brother died," she said. "On that fishing boat."

The boy didn't respond.

"I stayed with my neighbours in Vancouver to finish the school year, but now I have to live with my uncle."

The silence stretched as the boy bent low to peer again under the peony leaves.

Natalie made a fist and poked the plant in the space between her middle and index fingers. The spiral at the end bobbed forward like her uncle's dashboard Jesus.

"Why do you collect fiddleheads?" the boy asked, his face shrouded in the bush. Then he pulled himself up and squatted in her direction.

"Dunno. I like how they look."

"How's that?"

"How's what?"

"How they look."

She stuffed another fiddlehead into her knuckle. Its infant leaves wrinkly and balled into a bent finger. "Like a baby's fist," she said. She added a third between her pinky and ring fingers. "Or the end of an octopus arm." She added a fourth spiral, then looped her hand through the air.

The boy joined her on the tabletop and plucked a coil from her fist. He held it up to the sunlight.

"What's your name?" she asked.

"Milton. What's yours?"

"Natalie." She laid her three remaining fiddleheads in a palm-sized fan over the table. "Now, what's your secret?"

"Meet me tonight at seven?"

"Where?"

"Lane's Meadow. By the bee balm."

"Which is the bee balm?"

"The red ones."

ONE

Natalie found the first beads beside the tree trunk. Chinese porcelain—stick letters shaped like tents and Shanghai suns, inked below glaze. She had been scouring the forest floor for fiddleheads. The two beads sat on a bed of wet clovers and pine needles, and she collected them in her palm. Then she saw another a few feet away, and another, so she stuffed the baby ferns into the back pocket of her cut-offs and followed the beads off trail. The fifth was egg shaped and painted with a blue lily, and the sixth had a fishtail. The seventh bead, a crane, perched beside a pine cone on the edge of the crag. She pocketed it and searched the rock for more, wiped her fingers through crevices, lifted loose stones—and then she saw the cradle. It had washed up below, on a reef that tongued from the side of the cliff. Woven cedar, a broad hood, empty; the tide rocked it against the barnacles. A nut-brown bundle bobbed in the surf beside the reef.

She sank to her butt and shimmied down the crag, tennis shoes dangling, her fingers curled around grooves of stone until she could jump to the shore. She tiptoed along the reef to the bundle. When she reached it, she could not look. She stretched her hand toward the water with her eyes shut. Her fingers grazed a stiff stream of hair, then the blanket, which felt like wet suede, buckskin maybe, and she tugged it, bent into the surf to gather the bundle in both arms. She opened her eyes because it felt too light. Tucked inside was a cedar doll—lips painted with salmon eggs, a horsetail braid, and abalone eyes that shifted like oil puddles. She hugged the doll and felt her heart pound into the wood. She pretended it was the other way around.

Her canvas shoes were grey with sea water, and she felt something under her heel—an eighth bead. She spotted the spinning top after the next wave. A stringy bark cone pierced with a stick, which swirled in a puddle of yellow foam and sea ribbons. She rescued it and stepped into the water. The cold gnawed at her ankles, but she plucked through the seaweed for more items. Between crushed clamshells and pebbles she found something shaped like a thumb-sized boomerang, carved from bone and etched with black dots. She clenched it in her fist and gazed at the shore, at the trees that feathered from the cliff. That's when she saw the canoe. It jutted from a pine bough, and might have passed for a dead branch if not tilted to show it was a dugout. Natalie waded to shore and up the rocks until she stood directly under the canoe. Suspended in pine, the wood silvered, it looked like a vessel errant from Nod, swan nosed and lined with eiderdown, ferrying heavy-lidded children between dreams.

Roadnotes

SEPTEMBER 29

Spencer,

I have quit the library and quit town. My plan is to pursue autumn. To track the metamorphosis of deciduous woodlands. Where the leaf turns, there turn I. My first destination: the Laurentians. Mont Tremblant. La Symphonie des Couleurs. Southwest on Highway 40 to Montreal, then the Trans-Canada all the way up. From the Laurentians I will follow the colour south. The Green Mountains of Vermont, the Kancamagus Scenic Byway in New Hampshire, down, down, down, until pigment leaves the leaves, until winter strips the branches bare.

I have brought: a road map of the United States Eastern Seaboard, the *Complete Field Guide to Fall Foliage*, and Mom's lime MB roadster, which has not seen asphalt since the third impaired-driving charge. She told us if we had two pennies left in the world, we should buy a loaf of bread with one and a lily with the other. This is my lily.

Affectionately yours,
Sid

OCTOBER 1

Spence,

Yes, the colours are a symphony. I write from a ski suburb beside Tremblant called Petit Rocher. (I found accommodation outside town because town makes me feel trapped inside a Styrofoam city plan.) We are in what is called the "first wave." The yellow wave. Saffron leaves grope the birches like a thousand rubber gloves. Which reminds me—I found Mom's lambskin gloves on the back seat. The ones that snap at the back of the wrist, that she wore for "Sunday spins" around the countryside. What I remember is she never needed to remove them to count quarters for parking.

After a late lunch I poked around a Tremblant souvenir shop. They sell metal spouts and hand drills for tapping. The romance of the idea overcame me. I bought one of each, then drove for an hour until every tree was a sugar maple. (There is a chapter on tree identification in my fall foliage guide, with leaf silhouettes on the pages like ink blots.) I pulled over and selected a tree close to the road. The instructions said to drill on an incline for the sap to run down, so I did. Then I tapped the spout through the bark with the handle of my drill. I had forgotten to buy a collection pail, so I used my Snapple bottle from lunch. I was crouched nose to spout at the foot of the tree, Snapple bottle thrust under the tap, waiting for the thing to leak, when I heard a cough. A Hyundai had parked behind the roadster, and inside the Hyundai was a family of three. Their windows were rolled down and they stared from yellow, orange, and red visors. The woman in the passenger's seat (yellow visor) rested her elbow in the window frame and held binoculars. She told me that tapping season begins in February.

The Snapple bottle reminds me of my first and last ballet class, when I needed to bring a water bottle and we didn't have any so Mom sent me to the studio with an empty mickey of gin.

Next stop: Kancamagus Scenic Byway.

From Rocher with Love,
Sid

OCTOBER 3

Spencer,

On the drive to New Hampshire I tried to pinpoint the rupture of Mom's sanity. I couldn't. I think this means either A. she was born a lunatic, or B. wrongly committed. I lean toward A. Thoughts?

Reasons why A.:

1. She had an unnatural detachment from loved ones (you, me), and an unnatural attachment to American naturalism (the Helga Series by Andrew Wyeth).
2. After her alumni lecture at the Art Academy of Cincinnati she burned her collection in the school ceramics kiln (minus the sold self-portrait).
3. On our drive home from the lecture series we stopped at the Texas Snake Farm and she threatened to kill herself with an asp.
4. She poached eggs in cranberry juice.

I'm in Newport, N.H. The centre of town is an opera house, which I think is an idea that should prevail more in urban design.

Had to buy a fresh battery for the roadster in Montreal, but she's purred ever since. Also picked up a copy of the *Chronicle-Telegraph* and read the obituary. I liked how you began with "Once upon a time."

Living Free or Dying in New Hampshire,
Sidney

OCTOBER 6

Spence,

The Kancamagus Scenic Byway is a three-hour drive on a postcard. I arrive with the prologue to the second wave: leaves the colour of canned salmon. Clouds streak the sky like lawn mower tracks, and the air is warm and thick with the scent of fermented apples. En route to the byway I passed Santa's Village, which is home to an "electro-animated jingle jamboree" and a giraffe-sized drummer boy. Larger-than-life seasonal statuary discomfort me.

Do you remember the December we got the blue spruce? We returned from the ballet and she let me light the bottom candles, but when I stretched for a higher bough, my velvet jumper caught fire. You came running and she leaned against her armchair with eyes as grey and cold as nickels. On Christmas morning she cooked ricotta pancakes and poached pears, but for herself only took a cigarette and mulled wine from the night before. And on Boxing Day, she locked herself in the attic with the phonograph and *Madama Butterfly*, then emerged three afternoons later in her cotton peignoir and walked to the riverbank to collect snowdrops.

Honestly, Spence? That Christmas I wanted to buy her the asp.

Sidney

OCTOBER 7

I'm sorry I never went to the funeral.

OCTOBER 10

Spence,

Happy Thanksgiving. It's nine o'clock and the moon is sickled enough to hang a coat. I'm in Cavendish, Vermont, which is a town entirely unremarkable save for the man with a metal rod in his head. (Phineas Gage. Railroad worker, 1848. Google him.)

Dinner was a can of rice pudding from an AM/PM in Ludlow. The cashier had cream soda breath and Caesar bangs (you know the kind that bisect your forehead like saw teeth?), and when I made him break a twenty, he called me a "leaf peeper."

I can count the number of times she hugged us in the last two decades. Twice. Jean-Baptiste Day, 1990: I successfully smoke like a lady. March 1992: you get into her old art school.

Haven't reached mecca yet. (Mecca, for leaf peepers, is the Green Mountains.) I spent the afternoon driving through central Vermont, and skipped the World's Largest Filing Cabinet for a town named Barre (granite capital of America and source for most of the tombstones). In Williamstown I toured Knight's Spider Web Farm, which is run by a bald veteran with webs tattooed on his elbows. He cultivates spiderwebs, then sprays them white and lacquers them onto black boards. This kind of art makes me think that if you stare at the sun long enough, you'll see rainbows.

Tomorrow: Mecca. Then New York.

Never moon a werewolf,
Sid

OCTOBER 11

Spencer,

An hour into the Green Mountains I passed a blackcurrant bush and stopped the car in the middle of the road. The berries uneaten by birds were plump and overripe, and I peeled them in clusters from the vine. My lips and nails are violet with juice and it's the closest I've felt to gleefully carnivorous.

Some things I miss:

1. She cut apples width-wise so the core made a star.
2. She wore lipstick and never stained the glass.
3. She saved her watermelon seeds in a jam jar and tried several summers to grow her own patch.
4. She took milk baths.

On my last visit, she didn't speak. Not even when I told her you finished the sunflower series. And when I mentioned I had memorized all hundred divisions of the Dewey decimal system, she didn't even roll her eyes. You should have come with me.

I'm spending the night in Albany at a pie shop that moonlights as a motor inn. An elephantine sassafras grows in the parking lot. We don't have many sassafras trees up north. Their leaves have broad, rounded lobes that are layered like a wedding cake tall enough to conceal a stripper. I'm going to lie under the boughs and see if I can't get myself entirely buried.

Love Sidney.

OCTOBER 13

I'm in Auburn, N.Y. There aren't many leaves here, but there are crows, which from a distance look like leaves, especially when you cross your eyes.

There really are a lot of fucking crows. They line the chimneys and telephone wires and the awning of Curley's Restaurant opposite my window. The concierge says they arrived early this year. Every autumn since 1993, a murder of fifty to seventy thousand crows descends upon the ancient Aboriginal burial ground and proceeds to the town centre to roost.

They remind me of the baby crow Mom saved after Jacques-Joseph shot its mother with a pellet gun. Do you remember how she wanted to teach it to speak, so she clipped the tongue, and then it couldn't eat and starved to death? I think that incident neatly paraphrases our childhood.

The crows look finest when they fly. They take wing en masse and sweep through air like a hand-held fan. And when you bend your neck back to see only up, the sky looks like paper that a child has spattered with ink. The town hates them. They tear apart dumpsters and caw till the cows come home. And apparently by winter the volume of excrement is a biohazard. But I think they're magnificent.

She always wanted to move back to Ohio. Does it give her too much credit to believe we stayed in Quebec because she didn't want to uproot us? I think we should have tried harder for the health centre in Maine.

Guess what? The U.S. Department of Agriculture has activated a Fall Foliage Hotline. 1-800-354-4595. An automated voice informs callers of the country's colour peaks. The leaves in the New York and Pennsylvania Allegheny Forest should be exquisite. I head there tomorrow.

Unique New York Unique New York,
Sidney

OCTOBER 15

Remember the lightning storm that summer we camped on Lake Kipawa? Before the trees burned down, they were backlit by this glorious blaze. The trunks loomed scarlet and the colours were divine. Well, the sun glows behind the hickory trees as I write and the likeness is striking.

Are you familiar with the botany behind fall foliage change? In late summer the leaf's base develops a layer of cork that plugs its veins and prevents the entrance of moisture and minerals. Our Symphonie des Couleurs is a tree weaning its leaves off water.

Two weeks tomorrow is your opening. I hate myself for missing it. Good luck. Remember the liquor licence. Don't be nervous. The collectors will line up around the block.

Your Sidster (Ha, ha, ha)

PS—I think she was the most beautiful woman in the world. I think this is what redeemed her. She lived by a wild, unreasoned, breathless devotion to beauty. And not just her own.

PPS—My contact with humanity has officially reduced to you and muffler men.

OCT. 17

The bitch stole my boots! The pearl-coloured, full-quill, ostrich-skin Tony Lamas I won from the Montreal *Gazette*'s "Wild West" poetry contest in 1986! The pearl-coloured, full-quill, ostrich-skin Tony Lamas that vanished a month later, that I scoured the house for until the hardwood bruised my knees, that I just found in the original box underneath the passenger seat when I reached to find my fallen crust of pizza. I am parked on the William Flynn Highway, outside the Store Shaped like a Stealth Bomber, and I'm fuming in both French and English translations of the word. Will write more in Pittsburgh.

In Pittsburgh. I think the worst thing about our mother was the way she looked at us. She watched her children as she might a painting. Like she wasn't expecting us to stare back at her. And worse still, she watched us as *her own* painting. We failed because she was venomously self-critical. And worse than that, we failed because she did not craft us. You and I were the dice that spilled from chromosome Yahtzee, and how could that compare with Tarbell's *Mother and Child in a Boat*?

At least you went to art school. I think my decision to stack books for a living prompted her second relapse.

Tomorrow I try my luck in Tennessee.

Don't be bashful, Nashville.
Sidney

OCTOBER 18

Spence,

I opened the trunk. Which is to say, I spent two weeks in our dead mother's car *without* opening the trunk until three hours ago. I was "booting it" (they still fit) down the Pennsylvania Turnpike when the roadster met its ninth hole and burst its first tire. ("Pennsylvania: where winter eases driving because the potholes fill with snow.") I popped the back for a spare and found my: velvet riding helmet, patent leather Mary Janes, scarlet beret, flower press. Your: rock collection, private school blazer, clarinet, kaleidoscope. The buck antlers you found up north, a tambourine, and what looks to be the fourth floor of my Victorian dollhouse.

The roadster's at Esso getting refurbished. I've decided to spend a second night in Pittsburgh.

Sidney

OCT. 19

Spencer,

After two cups of jasmine tea, a bowl of won ton soup, and three hours inside an infinity of crimson dots, I'm going to Cincinnati. (In regard to the third point—there's an Infinity Dots installation at the Pittsburgh Mattress Factory.) No more bashful Nashville, no "Tennessee Waltz"; it's tin soldiers and Nixon on the I-70 to Ohio. I write from a hoisin-smeared booth at Lai Fu Restaurant, waiting for the bill and picking cabbage from my teeth with the fork my waiter gave me when he saw my attempt at chopsticks.

Do you think it's naive to believe her theft of our treasured childhood items implies a maternal sentimentality?

The bill's here. John Ruskin is inside my fortune cookie. I don't know what's odder—the quote's relevance to my travels, or the fact that an English art critic has replaced Confucius.

"Remember that the most beautiful things in the world are the most useless; peacocks and lilies, for instance."

Sid

OCTOBER 20

Spencer,

On the road to Cincinnati I passed three sunflower fields with flowers oily and yellow and spread-eagled beneath the sun, and then I passed a field of dead sunflowers, their heads bowed to the dirt like burned-out street lamps. (This fourth field would make a great finale to your set.) I passed a manor with a chimney and eaves that bled Virginia creeper, and then I passed the World's Largest Amish Buggy, and the World's

Largest Horseshoe Crab, and the World's Largest Apple Basket, and the World's Largest Washboard, and the World's Largest Crystal Ball, and the World's Largest Gavel, and the World's Largest Mortarboard Graduation Cap, and an animatronic Smokey the Bear. I alighted from the roadster at a chestnut tree near Lancaster and collected nuts in the front of my sweater. Then I stopped for coffee and a slice of cherry pie at a rest stop a few hundred metres away. But they didn't have cherry pie, so I ordered coleslaw and a burger, and the trucker on the stool to my left told me that what I collected were buckeye nuts, not chestnuts, and what I stopped at was a buckeye tree, the state tree of Ohio.

I spent last night at a Comfort Inn Over-the-Rhine. I aimed to be at the Academy of Art by now, but instead I'm on my third paper cup of coffee. What if they don't remember her? What if they have no clue?

Continued:
I met the academy dean, who sent me to the curator of the Childlaw Gallery, who sent me to the curator of the Pearlman Gallery, who told the student at the welcome desk to type something into a computer. So now I have an address for the patron who bought Mom's self-portrait, which struck me as a breach of privacy, but it's amazing how far you'll get with the right driver's licence and a death certificate. Our patron is "Ms. Izobel Moss" of Jerseyville, Illinois.

So. To Illinois.

OCTOBER 22

Spencer,

Five hours and the state of Indiana after my last letter, I pulled into a driveway littered with autobodies, a mile or so outside Jerseyville. At the end of the drive was a house the colour of a recycling bin. It looked freshly painted and under the sun gave the impression of melting. A chain-link fence enclosed a leafless pear tree, a plastic kiddie pool the same wet blue as the house, and a two-legged picnic bench angled between dirt and sky like a seesaw. A woman with three arms emerged from behind the tree. One swung against her hip as she walked into the shade of the trunk, the second was bent ninety degrees and perpendicular to the ground, and a third budded from that one like a flexed lobster claw. I asked if her name was Izobel Moss, and when she stepped from the shadow, her claw became an owl. A mid-sized owl the height of my forearm, with plumage like tweed and a chain that tethered him to the woman's wrist. She said, "Who wants to know," which felt so Hollywood that I said I had the ruby slippers, and she said, "Well, that's a horse of a different colour. Come on in."

Except that didn't happen. She said, "Who wants to know," and I didn't reply right away because she stood at the tip of the tree's shadow on the grass and really, really resembled its crowning Christmas ornament. Then the owl raised his wings and flapped, and flew the length of the chain and flapped, and hung suspended in the air like a helium balloon, and I said, "Sidney Marion. I think you bought my mother's painting. The self-portrait. She died a few weeks ago, and I wondered if I might see it." She didn't respond so I offered to show her the death certificate, but she said, "No need," and led me into her house.

And there she was. Our mother. In her ankle-length sealskin coat. You paint like her, you know. In the portrait, she wears a cloche hat, but her hair is slung over her shoulders, the ends corkscrewed and long enough to be stuffed into the coat pockets. I remember those pockets were deep enough to fit hardcover books and tins of licorice. Mom painted her skin pale except for the cheeks, which look rouged from the cold or physical exertion. Her eyes are cast toward the unopened umbrella she clutches with both hands, and her lips press together as if to keep from laughing. The portrait is exactly how I wish I could remember her.

I went back outside where Izobel and her owl waited for me on the porch, and without any sort of premeditation I asked to buy the painting. I hadn't planned to buy it. I didn't think I wanted to. I'm sure I didn't want to. She said it wasn't for sale. I said, "I'll pay you double." She said, "I don't need the money," and I said, "But she's my mother!" Then the only sound was the chortling of the owl. Izobel's eyes washed over me and she rotated the metal cuff from the chain around her forearm until her stare settled at my feet. "What size are your boots?"

–

Bitch steals my boots even from the grave.

I called the foliage hotline last week—reports for the Mark Twain National Forest look optimistic. I operate the gas in my socks because I can't find the shoes I brought with me. Mom rides shotgun.

Sid

OCTOBER 24

Spencer,

Mark Twain did not disappoint. Missouri's reached the third wave. Sweetgum and oak, black tupelo and elm: they all look dipped in ketchup.

Last night I bought three quarts of milk from the Hazelwood Grocery. I didn't know the optimum fat percentage for milk baths, so I got one carton of skim, one 2%, and one homogenized. I filled the tub with milk and hot water and rosehips I picked from the wild bush behind the motel. Now my skin is silk and I feel like Marie Antoinette, or Cleopatra, or our mother.

I miss you, Spence. If I leave tomorrow, I can be home for your opening. The Lost Maples of Texas will still be there next fall. And Mom would look fine in your studio.

Time to get my drive on Route 55.

Love Sidney

L’Étranger

After my master's degree in England, I moved to Marseille to let my hair grow. I lived with a Ukrainian woman in an apartment with stick-on floor tiles that peeled from the corners of the walls. I tried to not look at the corners too closely. Or the walls themselves, which were tacked with ribbed, oily paper. The apartment was ground level: when it rained, slugs slinked under the gap in the door. These weren't banana slugs from B.C., but slimmer and nut orange. Their trails shone in the glow of my cellphone when I walked to the bathroom at night. I used my cellphone for light so I wouldn't need to touch the walls for the light switch. Irina carried hers for music: Beyoncé while she cooked or bleached her underwear in the bathtub. I always knew where in the apartment she was standing.

Every week, Irina boiled potatoes on Monday, Wednesday, and Friday. She peeled the potatoes into the sink and left the skins in the drain. I had to scrape the peels to the side of the basin before I could rinse my lunch plate. Because I washed my hair on the same days, I started to see the potatoes as her detachable body parts. The potato halves like heels she unscrewed from her feet, or milky lobes she plucked from under her knees.

~

She had, let's say, certain tics. She hid dish detergent in the cupboard, though I bought a bottle when I moved in. She kept her own forks and spoons in a coffee can, her own sponge in a plastic punnet for grapes. I used to leave spare toilet paper on the tank, but the rolls disappeared. I moved the pack to my wardrobe. Every morning, I carried squares to the bathroom with me like a camper. Most days, we did not speak. She knew English—I heard her on the phone with her boyfriend. But she avoided the common rooms. When she accidentally entered the kitchen while I cooked, she walked around me to the kettle, then circled out again. Once, I sat at the breakfast bar and ate my couscous as slow as I could. I read the newspaper. I tried the French crossword. When I left, her bedroom door opened as soon as I tugged mine shut.

~

One day I sliced eggplant for a stir-fry. I had walked home from the market as it started to pour. The clouds blocked the sun like the pelt of a lint trap, and in the kitchen horizontal rain smacked the window glass. Irina opened the front door with her pale hair slick to her cheeks. She walked past the kitchen and switched off the light. She continued into her room. I paused. I could not see the eggplant well enough to guide my knife. I walked to the light switch and flicked it back on, then returned to my cutting board. I sliced eggplant. I would fry it with the garlic, ginger, and *cèpe* mushrooms I found at the market. Irina entered the kitchen with her hair in a towel. She turned off the light. She opened the fridge and removed a pot of yogurt and set it on the counter with a spoon from her coffee can. She left the kitchen. I flicked on the light. She returned in a bathrobe. She sighed and turned off the light and switched on the kettle. I sliced my eggplant in the dark until the kettle boiled and she poured her tea and left with her yogurt.

I think I started to hate her. She is the only person I ever started to hate. The internet jack was in her room, and she turned off the router at night. I bought her black electric tape to cover the lights, but that didn't work. I suggested she cover the router with a blanket. She said the router was loud. I said routers don't get loud. She said: This router is loud. She turned the internet off at ten thirty every night, which was her bedtime, and the time I wrote my emails. I lost approximately four emails.

Sometimes I came home and played music in the kitchen because there was no light in her window. But then I heard her voice on the phone, and realized she was sitting in the dark. Not to save bills. She showered three times a day, and every morning it rained she turned on the heat. Even though the temperature was thirty degrees outside. I would turn off the heat and go to my room. She would come out and turn it on. I would turn it off and stand behind my bedroom door and listen for her feet in the hall.

I do not know how the slugs got into the sink. I visited Marrakech for two weeks, and when I came home, the gastropods had harvested. I couldn't distinguish them from the peels: the skins plump and waterlogged, mired in gelatinous slime. The slugs narrow and orange like yam fries. Pan grease beaded the water that had not drained, and threads of chicken. A hard shell plugged the centre of the basin. It was either a snail or a peach pit.

The kitchen window was open. I had planted geraniums in the flower box on the sill. Perhaps the slugs came from there. But they wouldn't have mated if Irina had not clogged the sink with warm, organic matter. She must have been at school—I could not hear Beyoncé. So I opened Irina's cupboard. My eyes shifted from her spoon can to her sponge, her dish detergent to her chestnut spread. I considered what to do.

First, the sink. I emptied her utensils and scraped the slugs into the coffee can. I scrubbed the basin with her sponge. I wanted to dump the slugs on her bed, but she had locked her bedroom door. Instead, I opened her chestnut spread. I pinched a slug with my fingers and released it into the jar. When the body uncurled, I pressed it to the bottom. I added a second slug. I smoothed the paste over their eyespots.

She came home around six. I turned my music down so I could listen to her movements. I heard her set grocery bags on the counter and switch the kettle on. While the water boiled, she went to the bathroom. The hooks of the shower curtain clinked across the rod. She ran the taps.

I had tossed the other slugs outside, in the mulch of the palm tree planted in the courtyard. It was tempting to leave them in the can, with her forks and her soup spoons, but I did not want to kill so many. After her shower ended, she returned to the kitchen and opened her cupboard. I stood against my wall. I could almost gauge the weight of items she set down, but she restarted the kettle. The steam chortled too loudly. It was all I could hear. When the door tapped beside me, I jumped.

I waited until my pulse had calmed, then opened the door. She stood in the hall in bare feet, her bathrobe clutched around her waist. Pimples lit over her forehead where she had removed her makeup. Normally her skin was smooth as wax.

"Can I come in?" she asked.

Her fist trembled where she clenched her robe. I opened the door wider and she stepped inside. She sat on my computer chair. I did not know what to do. The sash of her robe dragged on the floor and I lifted it for her, but she did not see. It dangled off my palm like a braid of hair.

"Are you okay?" I asked.

She gazed at my computer screen, though the monitor had blacked.

"I think I found a lump."

"What?"

"On my breast."

I stared at her.

"Can you look?"

She stood and opened her bathrobe. I did not look down.

"There," she said, though she did not point.

I lowered my eyes, but did not know what to look for. Her breasts were larger than mine. That is all I saw. Two large breasts.

"Which one?" I asked.

She nodded to her right breast. I could not see a lump.

"I don't see anything," I said.

"Touch it."

"Touch it?"

"Underneath."

She gathered her hair to one shoulder, though it only fell to her collarbone and was not long enough to block my view. I leaned in and touched her breast with two fingers. I pressed gently. I could feel how cold my hands were.

"I don't know," I said. "I don't know how a lump feels."

"Lumpy," she said. She stared hard out the window like she might cry.

I continued to probe her breast, then felt it under her skin. The lump was small but firm, wimpled like the shell of a walnut. I lowered my hand.

"You feel it," she said.

"I'm really not an expert."

"But you feel it."

I nodded. She nodded too. She left her robe untied and walked out of the room.

In the morning, I cycled to Carrefour for a new jar of chestnut spread. I arrived fifteen minutes before the store opened, so I continued to the *pâtisserie*. I bought two *pains au chocolat* while I waited. When I got home, I cracked the seal. I removed spoonfuls of the new spread until its level matched the original jar. I tapped the spoonfuls into a bowl, then licked the paste off my fingers. From Irina's room, I could hear the furniture shift across her floor. It sounded like she was cleaning. I did not know if I should knock on her door with the *pains au chocolat* or wait for her to emerge. I did not know if we were friends yet.

After half an hour, she came to collect her underwear from the rack in the courtyard. She walked in the kitchen while I sat at the breakfast bar with my empty bowl. She turned on the kettle.

"Hi," I said.

She flinched at my voice and dropped the tea bag.

"Sorry," I said.

She bent to pick up her tea bag. She blew it off, then tossed it in the trash anyway.

"Pain au chocolat?" I offered. I slid the plate toward her on the table.

"No, thank you."

She retrieved another bag from her box. I paused with my hand at the end of the table. After a moment, I drew the plate back.

"I don't eat sugar before noon," she said.

"Oh."

I tugged the plate closer to me. I felt nauseous from the chestnut spread, but did not want her to think I bought the croissants for her alone. I tore a leaf off one pastry and nibbled.

"Listen," I said. "If you want someone to go with you to the doctor ..."

She looked startled again, as if she forgot I knew.

"No, thank you," she said again. She opened the fridge and studied the contents. She started to pull items off her shelf and set them onto the counter.

"Are you sure?" I said. "I wouldn't mind."

"Would you like my *crème fraîche*?"

"What?"

"It's nice with soup."

"Okay," I said. "Thank you."

She set the container on the table, next to my plate.

"I fly home today," she said.

"You're flying home?"

"Olives?" she said.

"Thank you. Why are you flying home?"

"I am sick."

"Have you seen a doctor?"

She shook her head.

"You should see a doctor before you fly home."

"I see a doctor at home," she said. "Plums?"

"Okay."

"Chestnut spread?"

I paused.

"It's nice with *baguette*," she said.

~

She left me all her food. She set each item on the table while I watched, as if otherwise I would not see. After she went, I sat before the mountain and felt I needed to eat everything. Like if I didn't eat the *crème fraîche* and plums and chestnut spread then, they would spoil. So I did. I ate until I could not eat, and then I sat on the stool with lead in my stomach. I wanted to retch, but could not bring myself to try. I stared at the containers, half-full of their creams, and the windows darkened. By midnight I could not see the food on the table, or even my hips, the lap of my jeans. I stayed until morning. I never bothered to turn on the lights.

Electric Lady Rag

At Japanese restaurants, Ilsa always waited for the booth with the cushions, even if it was only the two of them. Sitting on cushions set the peace, like the bamboo flute music and the water feature. Shoes off, heels tucked under her thighs, a warm mug of tea. That was her calm nowadays. The tea was important—the clasping of the mug, the nutty undertones. She had peeked under the lid once. They brewed the leaves with toasted rice. That was the secret, she told Dex. Boxed tea always tasted so acrid.

Dex was her sushi partner. If they didn't dine in, they ordered from Tokyo All-Nite on their work breaks. You didn't eat the fish at Tokyo All-Nite, or the pickled mushrooms, but Dex liked the tempura, and she could buy a vat of rice with sesame sauce for a dollar fifty. He was a DJ then. Now he was an "able seaman" about to be deployed to the Mediterranean. To mourn his departure, they went out for Japanese. But the calm was off. This would be his first time at sea for so long—nine months. He was nervous. His eyes flicked around the restaurant as though he couldn't remember why he was there. In response, Ilsa poured the tea before it had steeped. She burned her tongue. She poked the tip out and tried to suck air to it. Dex looked at her. She cleared her throat. She opened her menu and didn't glance up until she had organized three of the items into a haiku.

Salmon sashimi.

Mackerel maki-mono.

Eel yosenabe.

And so on. In town, Dex lived in a condo by the sea. She would move in after he left: to walk his dog and check the mail, and to flee her own roommate, who used drugs and her underwear without asking. She knew both of them from the Shangri-LA, where she danced and where Dex had spun songs before he joined the navy. She was a, you know, dancer, but she wasn't a, you know, dancer like her roommate, who traded extras for smack and left burned tinfoil on the toilet seat. Her shtick was vintage. Interwar grind house. Vargas girl sass, cute as a button, as a gal in a utility bra and silk stockings. She sewed her own costumes: feathers and rayon, sailor stripes sometimes, once a cigarette girl—tulle skirt and a pillbox hat. "Cigars, cigarettes, Tiparillos," she'd call, as she swayed under a wooden tray that hung from her neck. The music she danced to was mostly like heartbeats. Electric lady robo pulse. Strobe lights for optimal gyration. Anachronistic, but sometimes she'd soundtrack her own set. Droopy-sax jazz, maybe, or ragtime, if she wanted to bounce. "Louisiana Rag," "Mockingbird Rag"—flea-fingered piano you could swing to.

She sipped her tea and watched him read the menu. He held it like a newspaper, in front of his face with both hands, his freshly shaved head doming out the top. He had thin wrists and feminine knuckles—long fingers, like someone who played cat's cradle. Not someone who would report to work on a submarine for a nine-month game of all-or-nothing minesweeper.

"What if I break your leg," she said, a joke she had made before, but she wanted to end the silence. "I know self-defence. I could break your leg."

She sensed him pause, but he didn't look at her. "You couldn't break my leg."

"I know people who could break your leg."

"Ilsa."

"What if I'm with child." She slid her palm toward his elbow. "With your child."

He lowered the menu and stared at her, but his gaze seemed directed behind her. She withdrew her hand.

"Then I'd call you 'Mary,'" he said. "Mary."

There was an unconsummated tension between them. He had liked her at a time when she couldn't return his feelings. Now, too late, she liked him back.

"Want to split the soft-shelled crab?" he asked.

She didn't really. But instead she looked at the menu and pretended to consider the description. Her eyes drifted to the beverage list. You could buy a two-litre bottle of beer, which was twice the milk she kept in her fridge. When she looked up, he was still watching her.

"You go for it," she said.

"I may."

He shifted his knees on the cushion and peered over his shoulder at the server station. One of the girls saw him and hurried to their table. She wore a kimono, her waist cinched in a red sash. Ilsa lowered her eyes to the nigiri placemat—a laminated poster with pixellated food photos and tiny blurred font. She misread "fatty" as "city of." City of tuna. City of rainbow fish flesh. She wanted to show him this. *Look, Dex. City of tuna. Look at your placemat very quick.* But she didn't, because she worried he might not laugh.

He was at the club her first night. She was twenty-two and romantic enough to believe it was romantic. The bouncer asked for her ID. She said, "Hi. Hi, I'm new." The bouncer leaned into the door frame and shifted his eyes to the paper grocery bag she had carried her costume in. She withdrew a five-inch glass heel. "See?"

He shouldered the door open and told her the girls' washroom was downstairs.

The dancers' names were printed in red felt pen on the bathroom mirror, the first three ticked. Each name was clichéd—like the girls had drawn tags from a universal stripper hat. Ginger, Angel, Candy. Or alternatively: names with double *i*'s. Kikii. Kriis. Kiwii. Ilsa wanted a tougher name. A wrestler name. Like Rick. Or the Hacksaw.

"'Scuse," said a girl with latex elf ears. She leaned past Ilsa and ticked her name off the list. Brandii.

"Brandii?" Ilsa said, and folded her arms around her paper bag.

The girl turned. She tucked a breast inside her blue bikini top and lifted her chin to indicate she'd heard.

"How do I get my name on the list?"

The girl slipped a lavender shrug over her shoulders and stared at Ilsa as she did up the buttons. "Talk to the DJ. His name's Dex."

"Dex. Okay. Thanks."

"Change first."

"Oh," she said, then stared into her paper bag. She hadn't developed her vintage shtick yet, so her costume was silver spandex. Like a moonwalker. Or the Tin Man. She had considered spray-painting a funnel.

Dex worked upstairs in the sound booth. He wore a purple mohawk, his headphones crushing one of the spikes. She told him she was new and he didn't look up. He torqued a few knobs, then lifted one earpiece of his phones.

"Does the music sound tinny to you?"

"No."

He reached across the booth for a small whiteboard. "You danced before?"

"Well," she said. "I'm a figure skater."

He smiled. She continued, "And I've got a degree in linguistics."

Blue and green lights splashed across his face. He held the pen poised above the whiteboard.

"Stage name?"

She had given it some thought. She decided she liked cities.

"Tokyo?"

"Taken."

"Oh," she said, then couldn't think of her backups. "London" wasn't exotic. "Paris" set too high or too low a standard. She felt like she was choosing an email address. "Tokyo_64." She almost said that, but he was beginning to fiddle again with the soundboard.

"How about 'the Hacksaw.'"

His hand paused on a sound switch.

"Just call me 'Ilsa.'"

Her set started okay. She liked to dance. She hadn't bobbed her hair yet, and her lowest curls hung to the small of her back. She could helicopter her head the way she'd seen strippers do in the movies. The guys liked that. But she was nervous about the tip rail. About bending down to offer the first row her leg so they could slide bills into her garter, which she had secured with an elastic band. What if they didn't tip? Then she'd be bent over, alone onstage, her silver G-string glinting in the light lasers. So she stayed upright. She lifted her arms above her head. She tried to dangle from them, moodily. A trio of university boys started to laugh. It surprised her she could see them. She expected to be blinded by the front-of-house lights. She slowed, retreated to the pole. Realized she didn't know how to dance on a pole. She gripped it with one hand and sailed around like Gene Kelly. The boys laughed louder. Her cheeks warmed. She worried she would rash. Hives down her chest, between the triangles of her bikini. Dex said something encouraging over the microphone. A few patrons cheered. Someone tossed a bill. But she wasn't listening. She was slipping inside the beat. A remixed Billie Holiday song. All of her, why not take all of her. She could see her reflection in the mirror above the bar. How high her shoes were, transparent, so that she looked like she was floating.

When she got offstage, Dex bought her a ginger ale. "The

black lights," he said. "There should really be signs." He lifted her arm. Her deodorant was glowing.

"Oh god," she said.

"But plaque's the worst. At least you don't have plaque." He raised his glass, as if to say, *Here's to your teeth without plaque.*

Her mother had worked in the sex trade too. Well, she operated a switchboard. In the eighties, at an escort agency called Cloud Ten. She answered phones and spoke in code: "GFE," "open-minded"; described girls like paint swatches: hazel eyes, aquamarine. She had moved from West Germany when she was twenty-five, with a diploma in hospitality management. Her name was Freda. Friends and family called her Fritz. She had Ilsa when she was thirty. A young petite thirty, with small hard hips and breasts she didn't need a bra for. She kept her hair cropped above the ears; cut it with kitchen scissors, into a blunt lopsided fringe that hooked over her right cheek.

She never bothered with a babysitter. She baked bread. Spelt and sourdough. She left a fresh loaf in the oven whenever she worked nights. Ilsa sliced the bread herself. She would drizzle thick wedges with honey and reheat them in the microwave, until the honey seeped into sweet sticky snail trails she could plunge her finger into.

On Thursday and Friday nights, Fritz hung with the girls at Up Yer Alley Lanes. The decor was mid-century modern: drum lamps, fibreglass shell chairs, neon signs. The girls included three escorts, the other phone girl, and an aesthetician. A sixth worked at the laundromat, and another was a Yugoslavian shop clerk who sold Fritz a pair of Frye boots.

They would all settle into a lane, or a booth at the bistro, and order pitchers of beer and food puns—kingpin hot dogs, banana splits.

On Thursdays, Fritz worked the day shift, ten to five. She would meet the girls before she walked Ilsa home from the rink. If it rained, she cabbed. That was part of the culture. Cabs. Buses transported a different tier of prostitute. Fritz didn't escort, but she preferred to be driven from that place. The bus stop smelled like urine. Someone had spray-painted a penis over the Egg McMuffin ad, and over the penis, someone else had spray-painted a swastika.

Every cab driver knew the address. Some made comments. Others winked. She kept a list of safe numbers. Good guys who didn't care, who kept their hands on the wheel.

Some nights Ilsa didn't want her to leave. She refused to eat dinner, or hid the house key, or pretended to faint in the hall as Fritz searched for her boots. One night she elbowed her glass of milk onto the floor. She was eight, her hair cut short like a boy's. She stared at Fritz as she did it, her lips knotted. Fritz told her to get a mop. She said no. Fritz said, "Get a mop, or eat your Hamburger Helper."

Ilsa folded her arms and said, "I don't like Hamburger Helper."

"It's Beef Stroganoff. Eat it."

"I'm vegetarian."

"Fine. Starve." She opened the front door and waved her finger at the cabbie to indicate she'd be a minute.

When she walked back into the kitchen, she found her daughter on the floor, cross-legged in the puddle of milk. The girl squinted at her, arms still folded over her chest. "I'll clean," Ilsa said. "Watch me clean." She swiped a shard of glass from the linoleum and clenched it in her fist.

"What are you doing—you'll cut yourself!" said Fritz, and she ran to her.

Ilsa was staring at her own fist now, curiously, as though she had cupped a ladybird inside her palm and if she spread her fingers, it might fly out.

Fritz knelt in front of her, the milk soaking into her nylons. She laid Ilsa's clenched fist in her hand and whispered, "Open it."

Ilsa fanned her fingers one by one, and they both stared at the slice across her palm. The cut bloomed open into the milk, the blood streaking thick and pink like Pepto-Bismol.

Fritz kissed Ilsa's forehead. She hoisted her onto the counter, in profile, so that her small brown feet rested on the bottom of the sink.

"Lift," she said, and Ilsa raised her heels, plonked them on either side of the sink as Fritz ran the tap. She ran it gently, barely a trickle, and let it stream over her own hand until the water didn't feel too hot.

Fritz's mother, Ursula, kept birds. Passerines, from the city. She tossed seed onto the balcony and left the windows open. Birds flew in and out. House wrens and long-tailed tits. The occasional pigeon. A warbler built her nest inside the dining room light fixture. She and Fritz stopped using that light. They lit paraffin lamps. They rolled up the carpet and lined their armchairs with butcher paper.

Fritz's mother worked at a dress shop. Three nights a week, she danced between skits at a *Kabarett* called the

Fischglas. Her act followed a puppeteer from Munich, who left the stage covered in red paint. The posters called her routine "a leg show." She wore nude stockings and wrens tied to her wrists. "Ursula's Dance of the Doves," said the emcee, so she sewed white feathers to her brassiere.

She bought the zinc rings from a Danish birder at the *Universität*. He showed her how to clasp the rings around the wrens' ankles. She threaded them with fishing line, and looped the line to the silver bands she wore on her forearms. She would dance with four or five birds on each arm. Two or three perched on her shoulders. The others tittered at her cheek. In her hair. She sidestepped like an Egyptian—elbows out, palms flexed to the ceiling so the strings from either arm wouldn't tangle. The birds chirped and whined a percussion she could pepper her hips to.

Ursula ordered Sears catalogues from America. Every Sunday afternoon, before the food tokens, she sat on the balcony with her catalogue, a cup of coffee and condensed milk. She liked to see what the Americans wore. What combs they fastened in their hair. What undergarments, what springtime coats. Jumper frocks in the Paris manner, for breezy knees and locomotion, available in natural, Nile green, or coral. Fritz sat beside her and cut paper dolls. Wrens pecked at the seed. Crows pecked at the wrens. On the street, brownshirts assembled outside a delicatessen. A yellow-headed boy dawdled behind his mother, his fist latched to the hem of her Sunday skirt.

The Danish birder sent her a bouquet of amaryllises. He left notes in her mailbox—clipped letters of intent, written on university parchment: *Take lunch with me. I've brought fatty goose liver home from Paris.* Then, halfway down the page: *You are*, crossed out. Signed at the bottom. The Dane was ten or fifteen years her senior, but his face was boyish in a way that made him look thick. His smile curled around large, plate-like front teeth, and he parted his hair down the centre of his head. He spoke to her gently, and sometimes she couldn't hear him because he never raised his voice, even if they were at the club or the market on a Saturday, with the crowds and the fish hawkers. He was married, she thought, because he wore a ring, and when she asked, he pretended not to hear. A daughter too—the week before Easter they met at the market and he bought four papier-mâché eggs.

She needed money for her daughter's identity papers. Fritz's father was a Jewish actor from Kraków, who returned to Poland before Ursula realized she was pregnant. One of the bartenders at the club knew a guy whose daughter just died of tuberculosis. The girl was Fritz's age, and Catholic, and the man would sell the passport for one hundred *Reichsmark*. She couldn't count on her second income—the Fischglas would be closed soon; they all knew it. The sketches were too political. Last week, four officers watched the routines from the back. They didn't drink or smoke. They stood there like toads, between the toilet and the cloakroom. In his skit, the puppeteer's dummy wore brown khaki and patent leather boots. He stayed backstage. The costumes assistant snuck him out the rear exit. The pianist doubled the length of Ursula's song to fill time.

After the Dane sent the bouquet, she visited him at the *Universität*. His office was small, loose-leaf papered. The wood desk occupied most of the floor space.

He said, "Ursula! My day is brighter."

"I received your amaryllises."

"Oh—did you like them?"

"Yes," she said.

"I found a brooch yesterday. A pearl dove, with blue stones set in the eyes. It made me think of you. I wanted to buy it."

"My eyes are brown," she said, and smiled.

On his desk, a brass picture frame was angled between him and her so that she could see the face—a soft-cheeked woman with a limp bow tied around her neck. He followed her gaze and adjusted the frame nearer to his microscope, where he was examining a feather beneath a glass slide.

"I can't meet you this evening," he said. "But perhaps Saturday. After your show?"

She nodded, then paused.

"I need a hundred *RM* for my daughter," she said.

His smile faded. His eyes drifted to the lens of his microscope.

"I'm free Saturday," she continued. "We can take wine in my flat."

He nodded. She looked down. She hadn't had time that morning to press her skirt. She flattened a pleat with her thumb, then looked up again and rested her palm on the picture frame.

"She's pretty," she said, though she found the woman rather plain.

He smiled in a way that pinched his cheeks. Neither of them spoke. Finally he leaned over his lens and said, "A feather is one of the most elegant structures in nature. Want to see?"

She nodded and walked to his side of the desk. He withdrew from the lens so she could lean down. The feather looked like a disintegrated fern. The main vein was translucent and sprouting oily barbs, with tiny specks in the fibres like white dirt or dandruff.

"This one's from a Eurasian griffon," he said. "Beautiful plumage. You see?"

That Saturday night the puppeteer was arrested and the Fischglas closed early at 9 p.m. The Danish birder walked her home. Neither of them spoke when he followed her inside the flat. Fritz slept in her cot, in the corner by the stove. Her hair had loosed from its braid, and a crimped wisp of it lay over her lip like a moustache. Ursula lit the table lamp and poured two glasses of rye. The Dane hovered at the arm of the sofa. He lifted a corner of the brown butcher paper. It tore and he withdrew his hand.

"For the birds," she said. She slumped into a dining chair and bent over her knee to unfasten the strap of her shoe. The Dane leaned closer to the paper, then stretched his neck and sniffed.

"Is that ..." He indicated a spot of white with his chin. She smiled, and at that moment a pigeon ruffled its feathers from the shadowed corner of the couch and flapped into the air. The birder leaped back. Ursula poured herself more rye. The pigeon resettled onto the couch's arm.

"You keep them inside?"

He stepped farther from the couch and stuffed both hands inside the pockets of his trousers. She peeled off her second shoe. The twill of his pockets bulged as he flexed and unflexed his fists.

"Does it displease you?" She passed him his tumbler. He took the glass and sniffed the liquor. She scooped the pigeon into her thin bare arms and released it onto the balcony.

"Can we remove the paper?" he said as she returned inside. She stared at him, then swallowed another pull from her glass.

"The scissors are in my sewing basket," she said. "Behind you, on the floor."

He passed her the scissors. She kneeled into the couch and sliced the paper from the cushion in stiff, uneven cuts. He peeled the paper from his side and dropped a long strip of it onto the rug.

"All right?" she said when the seats were cleared.

"All right," he repeated.

She sat with her legs tucked beneath her and stared at the floor. He sank beside her and took the glass from her hand.

"Be quiet about it, okay?" Fritz was still sleeping in the corner.

He nodded and placed his hand on her breast, then slid it up, past her clavicle, into her hair.

UP YER ALLEY blinked the sign above the shoe counter. THREE STRIKES AND YER NOT OUT!

"Sevens?" said the boy who swapped shoes. He looked sixteen and well oiled, his hair slick to his forehead, a flush of acne across the bridge of his nose.

"That's right," said Fritz.

He smiled at her shoulder when she spoke, like a blind person, how they don't find your eyes, and he had a way of constantly nodding.

"I remembered." His eyes dropped to the tan leather boots she had plonked onto the counter. "I mean, your size is here," he said, tapping a boot. "But I didn't look."

"Those are eights, anyway," she said.

"They're nice." He tilted the shaft of her boot into the lamplight.

"Thanks."

"I can spray them if you like."

"What?"

"I have shoe spray," he said. "Anti-fungal."

"Oh." She looked down at her sock feet. "No, thanks."

"Okay," he said, still nodding. "That's okay." He took her boots and fetched a pair of blue-and-cream two-tones from the cubbies.

"So you're the first one here tonight?" he said when he returned to the counter.

"What?"

"Your work friends. My boss said you worked together. You're the first one here."

She glanced behind her at their regular booth. She'd hardly noticed it was empty.

"They're on their way."

Then at the same time she said, "How much do I owe you?" and he said, "Where are you from, anyway?" They paused. She said, "Berlin. The West." He said, "Two dollars."

"Thanks." She gave him a bill and walked away with the shoes tucked under her arm.

Twenty minutes later she sat with Mina, a barely legal "girlfriend experience." Fritz's bowling shoes were still tied together by the laces, balanced on the napkin dispenser between the ketchup and the salt. Mina ordered fries and soup du jour. Fritz ordered a root beer float. She sucked the foam through a thin red straw, and they talked about salad dressing. The merits of olive oil versus cream, how good it was for your hair. Your hair? Yes, and honey. Then Mina's eyes drifted over Fritz's shoulder and Fritz felt a tap on her back. The shoe-spray boy stood behind her with a slip of paper. She had a phone call. He read the name off the paper. From Ilsa. "Is she all right?" she asked. He bobbed his chin at her collarbone and said she could use the phone in the office. The call went like this:

"What's up, sweets—are you okay?"

"Can I go to Julia's for dinner?"

"Ilsa, this isn't my phone line."

"I found the number myself. In the phone booth."

"Phone booth? Where are you?"

"At the rink. It's juice break."

"Book, then," she said. "*Buch.* Phone book."

"*Telefonbuch,*" said Ilsa.

"Good girl."

"Julia's mom will drive me home after."

She told her not to be too late. When she hung up, the shoe-spray boy was smiling at her shoulder.

"Thanks," she said, and stepped past him.

"Wait."

She turned as he unzipped his jeans. He slipped his hand inside and withdrew his penis.

"How much?" he said. He thrust his pelvis toward her and searched for something in his back pocket.

She shook her head.

"How much," he said again. He tossed his wallet at her. It hit her shin and landed on the carpet.

She stepped away and navigated the space behind her for the doorknob. She didn't want her back to him. His penis was long and pink tipped. It lay stiff in his palm like a dead thing, an iguana maybe, or the iguana's tail. His hand curled into a fist around the shaft and began to beat back and forth.

She found the knob and swung the door open, pushed past the queue at the shoe counter, and ran through the glass doors to the parking lot. She bent over and breathed into her knees. Her toes in white socks curled into a pavement crack, into the dandelions that forced their heads through.

After sushi they sat in Dex's living room, on bar stools. He had bought stools when he moved in because he could carry four at a time. He didn't have a car to transport real furniture, and he said he didn't believe in paid delivery. Now she was moving in. She had packed her life into two trunks. One for costumes, another for civvies and books. She had brought her bed linen too, folded her sheets into a neat pile on the dining room table. It was the year of Our Lord two thousand and

Facebook. Tomorrow Dex would sail for Libya. Tomorrow she would swan-spin around the Empire State Building as Fay Wray and King Kong. He would wear a beret and his name on a dog tag. She would dab her palms with acetone for better grip.

"You want to see my new costume?" she said.

"I don't know." He fingered the collar of his wool sweater, which he still hadn't taken off. "I should pack."

"You haven't packed?"

"Well," he said. "Not my toiletries."

"Will you brush your teeth in the morning?"

"Yes."

"Will you shave?"

"Probably."

"Then you still need your toiletries."

"Fine," he said. "What's your costume?"

She'd got the idea from a burlesque performer in New York. A take on the old "Dance with the Devil" routine, where your costume divides vertically in half, and you wear a second head. Virgin versus Devil. Fay Wray vs. King Kong.

She unfolded the polyester fur from a bag in her trunk. She had bought it on eBay—kept the head whole, but cut the body down the centre with carpet shears.

Dex watched from his bar stool. He folded his lips. "Don't tell me you're a guerrilla fighter."

"No, but good one."

She changed in the bathroom, into a silk slip of a dress that detached down the centre by metal snaps. Beneath the slip, she wore a peach bra and hip-cincher underwear. She slid one leg into the ape suit, one arm, secured to her torso by Velcro and double-sided tape. King Kong's head perched on her shoulder. She could fit an entire unpeeled banana inside his jaw.

She opened the door with her gorilla paw because the suit was on the right side of her body. Then she clasped the paw with her bare hand and arched her back for a waltz. A Viennese waltz, down the hall, into the living room, spinning like a window display cake; a rotary dance, it's called, the Viennese waltz.

"Oh my god," said Dex.

She stopped and stood with both hands on her hips. "You like it?"

"Oh my god," he said again. He stretched his hand toward Kong's jaw, then withdrew it, like he might bite. "Does Terry?"

"Terry doesn't care as long as I'm naked by the end of the song," she said. "But I haven't asked about the Empire State Building."

Dex stood very straight now, with his hands behind his back. She wondered if this was at attention or at ease. Or if she could tell the difference. He'd become so temperate since he'd returned from training. Poised. Like they made the recruits balance books on their heads.

She let Kong's paw migrate over the fur to Fay's side, and maintained a neutral expression as his black, fur-tufted fingers spidered over her ribs. The paw cupped her breast. Her bare hand slapped it away. Kong stuffed his hand into his pocket.

Dex smiled like he was trying not to smile. "Chewbacca has pockets?"

"I sewed them. For props." She transferred her weight to one hip. "Bananas."

"Ah." He shifted his eyes from Kong's to her own. She could trace the movement in the dimples of his scalp, how they flexed when he clenched or unclenched his teeth.

Half her torso felt snug in the ape fur, but she was cold on the side of her slip, gooseflesh puckering her skin above the hem of her stocking. Dex wore his dinner shirt now, she realized. His navy sweater was folded over his sea boots at the door, next to her denim jacket, which he had also folded. She wanted to enfold *him*, she realized next. She stepped forward and pulled his torso toward hers, her arms around his back so that his armpit cupped her shoulder. His other arm circled her gorilla sleeve. Outside, you could hear the Saturday-night drunks laughing off the curb of the twenty-four-hour pizza joint, the shrieks of seagulls after their crusts. The living room bulb was dull, but light filtered in from the window, from the street lamps and rolling headlights, which grazed their shoulders toward the wall. Neither of them spoke. She wanted to stay here, in the hinge of this moment, before it tipped into the future or back into the past.

We Are As Mayflies

On the patio, my mother bets her boyfriend she can pour wine upside down. She drips wax into the ashtray and plugs a tea light in the wax. She pours wine into the ashtray and sets her glass over the tea light.

In the parking lot, Felicia Neufeld leans against the bumper of a dusty Jeep from Nevada. She licks her finger and carves messages into the rear window. WASH ME, she wipes. BITE ME.

In the blue room at the top of the house, my brother rows his ergometer machine. His shoulders tack forward. The flywheel eases into air from the fan.

I press the ion thruster and the Worldship blazes across the sky. With our improved navigational system, I steer our course toward the extrasolar planet 51 Osiris C. We settle on a moon rich in relevant natural resources, which we'll enhance through nanotech growth hormones and regenerative cosmic energy. Rapid construction and terraforming begin.

Two days in a row, my mother has forgotten to buy toilet paper. She bought SpaghettiOs and Pop-Tarts. She set the SpaghettiOs on the counter and said, I'm sorry, Gina. They were out of the Alpha-Getti. You'll have to practise your O words. O Canada, she said. O me! O life! Then she sang, O is the onliest number, and walked to the pantry with a stack of cans.

We've run out of tissue too, so I've left a roll of paper towel in the bathroom. But the towel is rough on my nose, and outside I am allergic to the microgametophytes of seed plants. I have begun to shoot my snot in the sink.

Felicia lives across the co-op in 208. She's not my friend at school because she is one year older, but last summer we mated our gerbils. Normally her hair is chlorinated blond, but last week she stole hair dye from London Drugs, and now it's as orange as Smokehouse BBQ chips. She has to wear a retainer. She's supposed to remove it before she eats, but she doesn't, and sometimes chips get caught in the metal bar. We ride bikes together. We ride bikes to the 7-Eleven to buy Slurpees, and we ride bikes to the school to drink our Slurpees in the basketball court. Grade seven boys shoot hoops in the court, and we ignore them. They ignore us too, except Scotty Lamb, who calls us lezbos. One day we collected gravel in our Slurpee cups. Scotty walked to us and said, Hey, Felicia. I wrote you a poem. Roses are red, violets are black, why is your chest as flat as your back? Felicia stared at her feet. She was wearing flip-flops. The Sky-Blue-Sky toenails we painted that morning had started to chip. Violets aren't black, she mumbled, but I think only I heard her. I felt embarrassed. I emptied my gravel over Scotty's head. Felicia lifted a bigger stone from her cup and threw it at his face, even though he was standing so close. The rock popped the lens out of his sunglasses.

My brother rows on the regional team. He and Mom have been arguing lately, so he keeps to his room at the top of the house. For Christmas, he got a television. He rows his erg in front of *Cops* and *$h*! My Dad Says*. His door doesn't shut all the way, and the light from his TV spills into the hall.

Aldo lives down the road from the co-op, in a yellow house between the 7-Eleven and a bluegrass field. He says he's fifty-two, but he has said that every year since I moved here, which was three years ago. Once my mother's boyfriend called him "the mongoloid," but my mother said he doesn't have Down's, and now my mother's boyfriend calls him "the mongoose." The paint on Aldo's walls is dry and splintered. You can peel strips of it with your nails. He wears a wool plaid coat and gumboots even when it's sunny, and his yard is overgrown with grass and dandelions and one papery, bruised hydrangea bush.

Felicia likes to talk to Aldo. She rides her bike to his house and lets him untie her shoes. He will pry off her Nike Shox Turbo runners and stroke the arches of her feet. Then he will slip a toonie in her sock and she will put her shoes back on and go to the 7-Eleven to buy Smokehouse BBQ chips or a Slurpee. She has asked me to come twice. She says it's fun. He touches your feet for only a minute and he pays you. The first time we tried we saw his sister's car in the driveway. We waited in the field and picked blackberries. The car was still there after an hour so we biked home. The second time he didn't answer the door, but Felicia opened it anyway. She coasted in on her bike and called his name, then leaned her bike against the wall under the coat hooks. I left mine outside and followed her in.

He's not here, she had said, and stomped into the next room. I lingered on the doorstep and wondered whether to remove my shoes.

Come on, she called. Sometimes he has cookies.

I followed her voice into a small damp den with wood-panel wallpaper, a Lazy Susan, and two corduroy armchairs. The room smelled like curtains and cold bacon.

What if he comes home? I said.

She shrugged and walked into the kitchen, flicked on fluorescent lights. By the time I followed, she was already on the counter in her running shoes, her underwear riding above her shorts as she reached into a cupboard. She slammed the door and opened another, scanned the boxes and cans until she found a tray of old Digestives. She took two biscuits and passed me the tray, which had no packaging except a layer of cellophane. I took two as well. She tossed the tray back in the cupboard and hopped off the counter.

We should go, she said. He might come home.

I followed her again through the living room, and she backed her bike out the door onto the porch. I was lifting my own bike from the gravel when I noticed her at the wood post with a Sharpie pen. She was drawing a penis. A horizontal penis, which looked like a blimp. When she finished, she snapped the lid on her pen and slid it into the waistband of her shorts.

51 Osiris C orbits every 29 solar days at a distance of .139 astronomical units from its parental star. Its mass is 2.8 to 3.9 times the mass of Earth and its radius is 1.1 to 1.5 times the radius of Earth, with a global equilibrium temperature of Ð47 to Ð22°C and a terrain that is pebbly. From its third moon, we shall install a silicate weathering thermostat, which will accumulate enough carbon dioxide in the atmosphere to permit liquid water to exist at the surface, provided the planet's tectonic composition can support sustained outgassing. My lab researchers have conducted a series of experiments on moist breads and clementines. Today we spotted our first zygospores. The oranges are moulding.

Felicia sits on a curb in the parking lot and watches my brother's window. I watch her from the futon in the living room. I don't remember if she knows which room is his. When she lowers her eyes, her gaze falls on me through the venetian blind. I open the front door. She's wearing cut-off shorts and a pink cheetah-print bathing suit.

Hey, she says.

Hey, I say. Want to come in for a freezie?

She shrugs and walks in, leaving her flip-flops on the mat, though her heels look just as dirty.

We only have orange and blue, I say, and head to the kitchen. I bring the box from the freezer and she takes the last blue. I select orange. We cut our ends with scissors and suck ice from the butts of plastic.

Look what I found, she says. She lifts a yellow bottle from her backpack. The label says lighter fluid. *Ideal for all petrol lighters and cleaning the home.*

Where did you find that?

Rob's shed.

Rob is the caretaker. He mows the boulevard and prunes the barberry shrubs in the parking lot.

Why were you in Rob's shed?

He left it open. Want to go to Aldo's?

With that?

It's nighttime—he'll be home. No construction on.

When Aldo's out, he's either with his sister or watching construction. There's a site down the road where they're filling the marsh with cement. Aldo watches through the chain link. The boom trucks and bulldozers, the orange men in their vests. He'll stand all day with a paper cup of coffee and sometimes a worker lends him a hard hat.

Come on, she says. I want a Slurpee.

I think about telling my mom or brother, but Mom's with her boyfriend, and my brother won't care. I grab my change purse. We walk because Felicia's dad took her key to the bike shed.

Why'd he take your key? I ask. Are you grounded?

She shrugs. She points to my Silver Surfer change purse and says, That movie was stupid.

I like the comic book.

There's a book?

Yeah, *Fantastic Four* #48, where they introduce the Silver Surfer in three issues known as the Galactus Trilogy.

Do you think 7-Eleven refilled the sour peach?

How I got into action comics is my brother gave me his entire collection of the *Fantastic Four* and *X-Men*. Most of the day he spends in his blue room, but in the morning he comes down for cereal and orange juice and I show him my experiments. Right now I am investigating the hydro cycle. I can produce rain with the tea kettle and a frozen spoon. For my birthday last week, I told him I wanted to be the first girl on the moon. He said they already sent women to the moon, so I told him I wanted to be the youngest girl on the moon, and he gave me freeze-dried Neapolitan ice cream and dehydrated strawberries. He said the first space explorers only packed food that fit into squeeze tubes, so the Americans ate applesauce and the Russians ate borscht. Borscht is a gory soup made of beets and cabbage. When I made a batch, my brother helped me with the blender. Then we funnelled the soup into a tube of toothpaste, which first we had squeezed into the sink.

At Aldo's, we speak to Aldo through the door, but he won't let us in.

C'mon, Aldo, says Felicia. Open sesame.

I can't, he says, in his voice that sounds like he bit his tongue.

I painted my toenails for you, she says, singing *toenails.*

My sister said to ignore you.

I brought a friend ...

My sister said you have to leave me alone.

Your sister's a cunt, she says.

I look at her. No one speaks.

C'mon, Aldo, she starts again. Aldo, c'mon.

He opens his door a crack and peers at us over the chain. He's got a squat pumpkin face, but all you can see through the opening are his eyes and flaky red nose. I smile at him. I want to leave.

Let's go, Felicia.

You owe me money, she says, and kicks his door, which slams closed.

I'll buy us Slurpees, I say. I brought my change purse.

You owe me, she says again. There are tears in her eyes.

Aldo locks the door, but I don't hear him move.

Felicia kneels to unzip her backpack.

Let's go, I say again.

She lifts out her plastic bottle of lighter fluid and squirts a figure eight over his porch. Before I can think how to respond, she flicks a lighter from her pocket and the figure eight ignites across the cement. It takes a few seconds for the entire shape to catch, and then the flames are ankle-high, and we watch the fire in silence until the fluid burns out.

We walk home without Slurpees. She doesn't say anything to me, so I don't say anything either. When we reach the co-op, I start toward my side of the parking lot.

Gina, she says.

I look at her.

See you tomorrow at 8 p.m.?

Okay, I say, though we never made plans.

My house, she says. See you.

At home, I stand outside my brother's door and listen to the breath of his row machine.

Dylan? I say.

Busy.

Can I come in, Dylan?

I'm busy.

His TV is on. I hear sirens through his door. Now silence. Now the clanging of a railway crossing. I go downstairs.

My mother's still on the patio with her boyfriend. She's blowing smoke rings. He waves the smoke away from his face with the back of his hand. From the futon, I see a small white face in Felicia's bedroom window. All the lights in her house are off, but her dad's Volkswagen Golf is in the parking lot. When I look again, her face is gone.

From the kitchen, I launch a bubble to protect the Worldship as we orbit a dying sun. I microwave a mug of hot chocolate. I carry the hot chocolate to the futon and worry about accelerated age.

The next morning, Dylan eats Apple Cinnamon Cheerios with apple juice instead of milk. I build a sink volcano and suck borscht out of a tube.

Choose a colour, I say.

Hmm?

Choose a colour.

Green.

Choose red or gold.

He looks up from his *Sports Illustrated.*

Gold.

I funnel baking soda into my Coke bottle and add thirty millilitres of glitter. In the measuring cup, I combine vinegar, dish soap, and yellow dye.

Count me down, I say.

Hmm?

Count down!

Ten, he says as he flips a magazine page. Nine, eight.

My mother shouts my name from upstairs.

Seven. He pauses. Six.

Gina.

Five, my brother says, ignoring Mom, slurping juice off his spoon.

When she charges into the kitchen, she's got my petri plate of zygospores.

This is what you do to the food I buy you?

She's wearing her soft nightie. The faded butterfly print that ties at the bust with two strings.

Four, says my brother. Three.

Hide it under your bed in my *pie plate*?

My brother snorts. When did you last bake a pie?

I can see streaks of self tanner around her armpit. I turn back to the sink.

Gina, your bread is growing fucking broccoli. We don't have money for this.

Two, one, zero, says my brother.

I don't move.

I said blast-off, he says.

I tip the vinegar into the baking soda. Gold froth shoots out of the Coke bottle, then burbles onto my sleeve.

He claps, then says to Mom, Why don't you go back to bed. Or did Mark leave?

Excuse me? She turns to face him. What does that mean?

Nothing.

No, really.

Dylan ignores her and returns to his *Sports Illustrated*. She continues to stare at him. He doesn't look up.

The baking soda is sodium bicarbonate, I say through the silence. The vinegar is acetic acid. The two chemicals join to form carbon dioxide gas.

Dylan stands from the table and tosses his bowl in the sink, which knocks over the volcano. Dregs of gold trickle out the Coke bottle.

My mother watches him leave. She grips the pie plate so tightly it shakes, the oranges wobbling in their sticky felt.

That's *Penicillium*, I say, and point to the mould. That's how you get penicillin.

I knock on Felicia's door at 7:58 p.m. She opens it right away, as if she were waiting on the other side.

Hi, she says. She's wearing her cheetah-print swimsuit again, with a netted shrug overtop. I take off my Green Goblin sweater. It's warmer in her house than outside, anyway.

We're out of freezies, she says. You want a fudge pop?

Sure.

She leads me into the kitchen, which looks like our kitchen, except with pale green tile. She opens the freezer and pulls out a box, slides it to me along the counter. I take an ice cream bar and slide the box back. There is a window screen on her kitchen table.

She leaves the box on the counter and lifts a pair of safety scissors. She slices a cut in the mesh.

What are you doing?

She smiles. You'll see.

I watch as she continues to cut the screen out of the frame.

Won't your dad get angry?

She shrugs.

But what's it for?

She peels the screen from the frame and holds it in the air.

I said *you'll see*, she says. You like experiments, right?

With window screens?

She shrugs again and rolls the screen into a cylinder. She tucks it under her arm and doesn't explain even as we walk to Aldo's.

He's in his driveway when we get there, inflating a bicycle wheel with a hand pump. He looks up when he hears our shoes on the gravel.

Oh, hi, he says.

Hi, Aldo, says Felicia. What are you up to?

He shrugs, lets the handlebar of the pump drift up. Just some handiwork.

Cool, says Felicia.

I smile at Aldo when he looks at me, then drop my eyes to the ground.

I brought ice cream, says Felicia, and she pulls the box of fudge pops from her bag. We better put it in the freezer before it melts.

Aldo glances at his front door, then back at his bike tire. I don't know, he says.

We better put the ice cream in the freezer before it melts, she says again, and walks past him toward the door.

Well, all right, he says, and hurries in front of her, opening the door before she can.

Felicia smiles, kicks off her flip-flops before she walks

inside. She grabs my wrist as I pass her on the porch. Get the screen, she whispers, and I see it's still there with her pack on the curb.

When I return inside, Felicia is sitting cross-legged on one of the armchairs, rocking back and forth until the chair reclines and the footrest springs out. She laughs. Aldo hovers between her and me in the front hall. The fudge pops have been tossed onto the coffee table.

Aldo, get a bowl from the kitchen, says Felicia. Not too big.

He doesn't move.

Gina, can you pass me the clay?

The clay? I say.

In the pack.

I think you should leave, Aldo says.

I hug the pack to my chest and remain where I am.

Aldo, will you please bring a bowl?

His brow creases and a whine murmurs from his throat as he looks over his shoulder toward the kitchen. Then will you go?

Yes, Aldo. She smiles and plucks herself off the chair, walks to me across the rug. She tugs the pack from my arms and snatches the screen from the floor. I realize I've forgotten to remove my shoes.

Aldo shuffles to the kitchen and returns with a glass mint dish. Felicia's seated herself on the Lazy Susan table and works a ball of red Plasticine in her fist. He winces at the sight of her on the table and looks to me. I avoid his eye contact. Felicia presses the Plasticine into the rotating wood disk of the Lazy Susan.

You tracked mud inside the house, says Aldo, and it takes me a moment to realize this is addressed to me. I look down at my shoes. There's a chunk of dirt on the heel, but not enough to transfer onto the carpet.

Felicia smiles. She's wrapping the screen around the wheel, securing it to the wood with duct tape.

I kneel down to untie my laces. When I look up, Aldo is staring at my feet.

I'll need a rag, she says.

An embroidered handkerchief pokes out of Aldo's breast pocket. She hasn't noticed yet—she is reaching inside the mesh cylinder to press the bowl to the Plasticine. It would have been easier the other way around.

The longer Aldo stares at my feet, the more I feel alienated from them, as though I could not wriggle my toes if I wanted to. My feet are moths, I think, pinned into foam, and Aldo is my dumpy lepidopterist, a word I learned last week. Before I have time to think it through, I reach across the table and tug the handkerchief from Aldo's pocket. I pass it to Felicia. They both look up, surprised. I know I have impressed her. A thrill blooms in my stomach like a small smile.

Felicia squirts a stream of lighter fluid into the rag. She releases the rag onto the mint dish.

Shall we sit? she says, and climbs off the table, offering me a chair.

I sit where she gestures, left of Aldo.

Felicia kneels in her own seat, straightening her shorts over her thighs like how you arrange a napkin. She strikes a match from her pocket and drops the flame into the cylinder.

We both flinch as the rag catches. Beside me, Aldo emits another low whine.

Felicia lowers back to her calves and smiles at me from across the table, her cheeks auburn in the firelight. She lifts her hand from her lap and spins the Lazy Susan. The flame grows as the wheel rotates faster, fire spiralling as tall as the screen. And it's beautiful. The heat twisting like a supernova as it collapses and expands.

Then the bowl explodes. Shards of glass shoot from the screen, and for a moment that too is beautiful. But all of us scream, kick back the chairs, and shield our eyes.

I wait a few moments before I look up from my sweater. Aldo has dipped under the table, clutching his forehead. With the Lazy Susan no longer spinning, the fire has shrunk. Felicia rises slowly from behind her chair. The screen wings out from the tape, and Felicia and I both wince back, the mesh drooping over the wood. Felicia lifts the leather cushion off her chair and tosses it over the remaining flame. We stare at each other. I can hear Aldo trying to be quiet as he cries. When he lifts his face, a stream of blood trickles down his temple.

We leave then. Felicia rips the screen off the table and grabs her backpack and the lighter fluid. On our walk home, she tosses the screen into another co-op's dumpster. I don't mention that we left behind the fudge pops.

At night, I am restless. I dream of a calm tomorrow spent navigating Osiris. I can hear my brother's erg when I get a glass of water. I sit outside his room and watch him row in the watery light of *Law and Order.* His back pumps forward; his knees flex into the gush of the fan. It looks like his strokes power the television.

The next morning is Monday. I pack space food: dehydrated strawberries, freeze-dried Neapolitan ice cream, a tube of applesauce, a tube of borscht. My brother eats Coco Pops in coffee. I ask him how astronauts drink hot beverages in space.

Zero-gravity cups, he says.

I don't own a zero-gravity cup.

He shrugs. Use a straw?

So I pack a juice box. It's a fresh honeydew morning, and I walk to the construction site along the drainage ditch. The marsh is gated off with chain link. Through it, you can see the machines groan over dirt, their slow scraping of mud and tall grass into mounds.

I don't see Aldo at first, but I hear his voice on the other side of the fence. He sits ten feet in front of me, on the upturned shovel of an excavator. A woman sits next to him. I crouch between the gate and a sedge bush.

The woman has thick, hedgy hair combed into a braid. Her blazer is creased at the back, but she's wearing nice shoes. Pumps, I'd call them. Leather pumps, perched on the edge of the shovel away from the mud. She and Aldo sip from paper cups.

That's an articulated hauler, I hear him say. He points at a dump truck with a load of sand. The truck starts and stops, flashes its tail lights and reverses toward the gate.

I open my applesauce and squeeze a dollop onto my thumb. It smells minty.

See that? Aldo says as the woman stands. That's a knuckleboom loader.

She folds closed a box of donuts and passes it to him. Knuckleboom? she repeats, and I say the word too because I like how it sounds. *Knuckleboom*.

Guess how much it weighs? he says.

The woman shades her eyes and looks toward a truck mounted with a protracted metal crane.

Five thousand pounds?

Sixteen thousand.

Well, that's more than you.

Aldo laughs. She bends to collect their creamers and napkins.

Need any more serviettes? she asks.

He shakes his head. Ahead of them, the dump truck unloads its sand.

I'll drop by tomorrow? she says, and he nods. Four p.m., she adds. Tea time.

She turns and picks her way to the gate, the heels of her pumps sinking holes in the grass as she lunges across the mud patches.

Bulldozer, Aldo says, even though she's gone. Eleven thousand pounds.

The bulldozer rolls toward us on its rubber tracks, its shovel pushing a mound of wet dirt. They're carving the marsh into a crater—the excavators like moon diggers or lunar trenchers, though the way they clang their necks in the mud they look like bathing birds. Ahead of me, Aldo shifts to adjust his trousers. As he settles into a more profile position, I see the gash on his temple has been basted closed.

I am alarmed by how the sutures are not neat. The thread tacks across his skin from all directions, like he stitched the cut himself. I wonder if he did. Then—I cannot help it—I wonder what needle he used. If after we left that night, he stood in the bathroom mirror with a spool of his sister's thread. I had brought enough food to share, but now I do not want it. I want to leave, but cannot convey that message to my knees. Ahead, Aldo crumbles a donut between his fingers and licks his thumbs. I watch him as he watches the machines.

Missing Tiger, Camels Found Alive

A truck and trailer containing a caged tiger and two camels were stolen from a motel parking lot near Saint-Hyacinthe, Que.

—CBC News, June 18, 2010

On the curb smoking Florida cigarettes while my love sleeps in at the Honeymoon Motel. Kilometre three thousand of who knows, en route to someplace sunny: a riverside mobile home, maybe; or honey-walled single bedroom on the south side of town. Someplace where happy-hour daylight throws rainbows from the suncatcher prism I bought my love when she told me she was pregnant. I promised her premium lace curtains and a two-car driveway to start—then all the plains in Spain and the express lane out of Ontario. Crowned Miss Mississauga in 1996, she's accustomed to finery: to salon tans and expensive bathing suits. She drinks white wine with ginger ale and reminds me to use a coaster. She plays croquet, always yellow, and I want her for my wife.

The motel parking lot slopes, and I'm watching a shopping cart roll toward the road, when I hear a growl.

Feline and guttural, too baritone for anything domestic, emerging from the Ford parked on the other side of the lot. Logic says someone's in the attached trailer, too cheap for a room, their snores plangent in the pre-commuter silence of Sunday morning, six a.m. It's when my arm hairs shiver that I investigate—some sixth sense from the cave that recognizes beast when it sings me in the ear. The growl sturdies as I peer inside the truck window, cabin empty, and walk the length of the trailer, a boxy aluminum submarine with four soft-edged windows on either side. I find the camel in the first window. Long lashed and schnozz like a sock puppet. Then another, bowed for a drink at the water tank. Blinds down on the second window, and open only an inch on the third. But it's enough to see two fat algae-coloured eyes, heavy lidded and blinking in quarter time. Stripes haloeing the burnt-orange fleece of its cheeks. Salty chin shifting toward me; eyes catching sunlight, glowing like mirrors.

I stole a tiger and two camels from the parking lot of the Honeymoon Motel because royals keep big cats and I'm in love with the Queen of Central Ontario. Because when you meet a tiger, you know it's closer to God than anything that wears shoes. Because Miss Mississauga should see her majesty reflected in something alive, and she's as wild as they are. The type of girl birds perch on: no seed—just a book, a park bench, and clavicles for landing. In fact, that was the talent portion, which she danced to Édith Piaf. I remember her palms and a top hat of hummingbirds, green orbs launched into wash lights. They returned at her whistle, abuzz at her wrists before Piaf got to the line about *mots de tous les jours*.

Truly, the recording's on YouTube. I figure it's genealogical. Her dad trains the hottest quadrupeds outside L.A.—the guy off-screen coaxing the tiger with beef jerky.

It takes less time to hook the trailer to the station wagon than it does to coax my enormous queen out of bed. Supine in the polyester bedspread like an Eastern fertility goddess, full bellied and sublime. Beach-bleached hair she can sit on, voluminous with yesterday's mousse and last night's dreams. I say, "Blanche." I say, "Wake up." I say, "I've stolen a tiger and two camels."

"Fuck off."

"We have to leave. We're on the run. I checked us out."

She rolls over and tugs the comforter over her head.

"Seriously," I say.

"Seriously fuck off."

I tug the string on the venetian blind and sun filters in anticlimactically.

"Blanche." The echo of piss in a rented toilet. "Darling?" I turn to find the bed empty and sheetless. The toilet flushes and she shuffles into the bathroom doorway, loosely cocooned in three layers of blanket.

"Get dressed," I say, and collect odds and ends. My penguin tie, buck fifty at the Sally Ann, her nylon socks slung between the antennae of the TV.

"I think my tongue's swollen."

"Ten seconds." Stuffing my tie and her socks into the suitcase. "Nine."

"Put a run in those and you're dead."

"Eight."

"Duh ih looh swo-en?"

"It's not swollen. Put this on."

"How do you know?" She climbs into the sundress, shimmies it over her belly, the white cotton bodice still gaping at her bust.

"You can talk."

She frowns and fingers loose a tangle in her bangs.

Let's begin with the dandelions. How they linked each wicket by dusty stems. The girlfriend of the postgrad golf star plucking them before the players could descend their mallets—a waste of wishes, she explained.

"Like pissin' on four-leaf clovers," I said from the iris bed, garden spade tapping the chipped hood of a gnome.

"Right," Blanche said, wet lips softening. She was three months pregnant then, though she didn't look a day over well-endowed.

Her beau ignored me and said to his colleague, "How charming she is. These hang-ups. Last night on the patio she insisted we dine in the dark because the torches were incinerating the moths."

Blanche winced at *incinerating* and bowed over a dandelion, sank into a crouch that made the two of us level. She plucked the stalk and shut her eyes, hovering the weed at her chin for an inhale, eyelids chalked a gentle green and quivering. She tightened her mouth and blew, the seeds bursting off the dandelion and riding my way on the shape of her breath.

"Blanche. Your stroke."

I clasped the filaments in my fist, cast my own wish and whistled them on. The seeds piggybacked with double requests, but weightless and illumined off my palm like particles of lamplight. Blanche grinned before she stood, one of her sash-and-crown smiles. Then she left me to garden by the path of their croquet course, to linger behind the delphiniums, digging and filling idle holes. After their game, she told her boyfriend she might like cranberry-walnut sandwiches for lunch at the faculty club. I prefer to clean the language departments—the pretty, plump secretaries dialoguing *en français—la photocopieuse*—or Russian, even better—"Fine day," I might say, the assistant from Moscow nodding with breathy *da*'s. Foreign languages fit women like low-cut tops, and me, I like to play spy, pretend to pretend I'm a cleaner inside the United Nations. But that day Blanche's desire for cranberry-walnut sandwiches had suggested the windows needed washing at the faculty club.

She sat between the guard dogs, attending more to her ginger ale than to table talk. The boyfriend moving his lips more than any of them, frequently chuckling, pleased at his own pithy revelations, not looking at the waitress as he ordered: tea, no sugar, probably—cucumber sandwich, no crust. Suds slopped down my windowpane, the soap fanning over glass, my view of the table filtered through a glycerol prism—Blanche tinted the colour of free love and Jerry Garcia. I whisked my bucket of cleaner and spread the froth on my pane for fingerpainting: *.dehs eulb eht ta em teeM*

She didn't see the note. But she caught me later to report the dog feces I'd been avoiding, and to find a hose for her pumps. I worked the tap, held her hand as she stood on one foot, and she agreed to milkshakes the next day at the student union building. That's the date she told me she was pregnant.

The boyfriend didn't know for another month, after we'd had six more milkshakes at the student union building. She told me other secrets during those sessions too. She said she never met such a good pair of ears. Eyes, yes. She'd met lots of eyes. But they don't understand so well if you don't know sign language. When she told her boyfriend about the baby, they argued for three weeks and she cancelled our afternoons at the SUB. I brought a vanilla shake to her house and she answered the door with a red upper lip and bloated eyelids. She mentioned a pageant pal in Florida, and I was happy to get away myself.

Zero klicks an hour on the shoulder of Autoroute 20: Blanche warms to reality. To the regality of our captured tigress. The trailer is idled between happily ever after and the parking lot of the Honeymoon Motel. We're at the open side door, the tiger glowering from its cage, pupils shrinking, haunches clenched in the air.

Blanche shifts her gaze to me—eyes alert and unblinking. "You're a lunatic."

"Now, darling."

"Like, clinically. Like Call The Number On The Screen."

"Hush," I say, and reach to pinch the lint from her sleeve.

She smacks my hand away. "You stole live zoo animals. We can't leave them now—do you *get* that?" She continues to stare at me and I'm not sure if her inflection is rhetorical. "You think we can get back to the entrance and rehook the trailer before the original driver comes out?" She looks from me to the tiger. "And if we could, then what? I don't want to be the one who sends them back to the zoo. They trade these guys like hockey players." She hoists herself onto the aluminum and crouches before the cage.

I think about responding, but she continues before I can think of how to word it.

"His eyes look milky," she says. She leans closer, her nose an inch from the crate. "And look at the missing fur up his arm." She sinks her head closer to the paw, its limb stretched across the aluminum like a log. "I'll bet they Vaseline his teeth before showtime too."

The cat socks a cheek into the cage and navigates the bars with his gum. I can hear hoofs knock about from the next compartment, then a flank swipe into the divider screen.

"Look, we were headed for Toronto," says Blanche. "What if we kept north for my dad's cabin?"

"Anywhere you like," I say. But I've seen photos of the ranch, and that is exactly where I want to go. Miles from no place, bordered by butternut trees.

"The property's huge," she continues. "And he's handled wild cats. He'd say no if I called. But maybe if we just showed up ..."

Her Majesty, the Queen of Central Ontario, barefoot in the sweetgrass. Hip to hip with her dozy cat.

~

Miss Mississauga. M-I-S-S—I-S-S. Miss Mississauga sucking grape slush through a too-skinny straw.

We're doing a hundred because I'm pissed off. I tried

to feed one of the camels a carrot and it bit my thumb. I'm about done with them now. I'm about ready to let them off at a rest stop.

"Jeremiah?" Blanche says, the Quebec visitor guide opened on her knee.

"She might be a she."

"You'll have to check."

"Cleo?"

"Cliché. Hezekiah?"

"Heze-huh?"

She lifts the guide and thumbs it like a flipbook, cover to cover.

"Tonight let's stay someplace with a pool," I say.

She glances at me from the book. "You don't think we can make it to Ontario?"

"Not with rush hour traffic. And there are nicer motels in Quebec," I say. I don't tell her the last thing I want to do is drive all the way to Ontario. The car stinks. I can smell the camels' shit from in here. Or maybe it's coming from my shoe.

"Well, I think we should try," she says, and stares at the windshield.

"Plan B hotel, just in case?"

She sighs. "What city?"

"Whatever city you like, my darling."

"Drummondville?"

"Sounds pretty."

"Or a shit hole." She turns the page. "Motel Alouette—'warm and discreet atmosphere.'"

"Discreet," I say. "Perfect."

"Or hourly," she says.

"I think I have shit on my shoe." I lift my foot from the brake pedal. "Can you see?"

She shields herself with the book and continues to read.

"I don't see anything."

I lower my foot and glance in the rear-view mirror at the trailer. I can't help but wonder, of course, if tigers eat camels, given the opportunity. Stranded on the shoulder of Autoroute 20.

"Hey, a horse show," says Blanche.

The trailer door left carelessly ajar while Blanche and I pull over for lunch.

"I haven't seen a horse since I helped train Popcorn for the close-ups in *Seabiscuit*."

Divider removed. Nature and Darwin resuscitated: a tidy denouement. Though perhaps unethical. Upsetting to the Miss.

"What's the date today? The seventeenth? Take the next exit. Right here, Richie. Turn right here."

Exit 181 at Saint-Joachim-de-Courval. We enter the stadium by way of the sale stables—twenty grand for a Bavarian Warmblood sired Cornelius Rottaler II; thirteen grand for Sheeza Lady, the Welsh Pony next door. The stalls fortified by barrels of oats and barley. Grass bales. Cubic pyramids of alfalfa. We've found the mess hall, then—surely camels eat hay? Perhaps if we drop them here at a feed station, flee before security spots the humps.

Blanche has sealed her hair beneath a prodigious sun hat. She might fit in, were it not for the road-wrinkled dress and third-trimester sweat glinting between her shoulder blades. She points to the dressage arena and loops her arm through my elbow. I follow her to the bleachers.

A British announcer booms over the PA—*"the sensation really"* (rehlly) *"of today's competition"*—as though druh-sahzh requires Anglos shipped from the motherland—*"eight- year-old Lipizzaner stallion, Neapolitano Magnifica."*

"Isn't it awful?" says Blanche. "How they're paraded. I wish we could save them too." She tugs my sleeve toward the front benches. Neapolitano Magnifica glows in centre ring, white coat tossing the sun beneath my eyelids. I can't look straight on. He's beatific. Flawless coat, as if before showtime the rider rubbed any imperfections with wet chalk. Vaseline for the chomps, perhaps. He trots in place, ankles springing like they're hoofing on toothpicks

"How supple his back," murmurs the announcer, "*a cadenced* piaffe."

A cadenced *piaffe*. Édith Piaf. "La Vie En Rose." Supple backs and regulation heels—toothpicks, minimum 7.5 centimetres, she said. Blanche, *ma rose*.

"Blanche, my rose," I say. "I forgot something in the car. A couple things. I'll find you in twenty."

Blanche's wrist slides from my elbow and I barely catch her smile before she drifts toward the front bench.

"Just look at the height and the freedom in front," the announcer rumbles as I slip back toward the trailer.

Operation Camel-y Freedom. The trailer air is thick with unventilated piss, and here's me, hunchback of urine can, sweet-talking the beasts from the collar of my T-shirt. I make lip-sucking noises, cluck my tongue.

"Out you go, boys—all-you-can-breathe oxygen, I promise you that."

The camels are impervious—not negotiating. I gently shoulder-check one toward the open door.

"C'mon. Go get yerselves some vitamin D."

What's that they say about camels and stubbornness? I glance out a window, then face the nearest brute eye to eye. His face is like how children draw cats—anchor-shaped grin dropped from a triangular nose. I think he's laughing at me. Perhaps they expect remuneration. Food-like.

Behind the sliding steel divider I can hear the tigress pacing her cage. She'll be getting antsy soon too. Outside the trailer, the nearest food I see is a barrel of barley pellets, so I jump out and stuff my pockets. When I climb back in, one of the camels faces me straight on. The other stands sideways, bending his hind legs for a stretch. Both camels are single humped, fur the colour of toasted oats, spines arching up. I wave a handful of pellets under the nearest guy's nose and back slowly toward the door. The bent camel snorts, and that starts the one opposite me, who works his jaw like now he's about to spit.

"All right, assholes. Get out or I'm going to find you each a piece of straw."

The tiger's groaning. Diaphragmatic whines that reverberate down the wall. Then a roar—thin from the roof of the mouth, resounding deeper.

"Headed out?"

My love stands at the trailer door. She shades her eyes with one hand and holds her belly with the other.

"I found pellets," I say, and let the oats slide through my fingers, palm still outstretched.

"You were leading them outside."

"Well, I figure we couldn't ask for a finer dead drop."

"Dead drop," she repeats, her syllables slow and evenly accented.

"For the camels. I guess I don't see them at the ranch."

"Ranch," she says. Then silence. She stands very straight—pageant posture, sternum lifted. Her stare shifts from me to the camels to the folks at the stalls.

"Listen, Rich. Let's see how far west we can get by sundown."

Eighty klicks an hour on Autoroute 20. Towing wild cargo. Call me Frank Buck. We made headlines. I caught the glamour shot of our tiger on the front page when we stopped outside Drummondville for gas. TRAILER WITH TIGER, TWO CAMELS STOLEN IN QUEBEC.

We say nothing as we leave the station. Blanche marches ahead, juggling travel wipes and a bag of corn nuts as she manoeuvres her belly into the passenger seat. I take my time, slide behind the wheel a few moments later. Her eyes stay locked to the window, travel wipes and nuts still cradled in her arms.

"They didn't include the plate numbers," I say.

"No. But the trailer make."

"Fear not, love—"

"Just drive, okay?"

"We're heroes, you and I. That's what's missing today: heroics. Gone are the days—"

"Why are you still on the 20? We should be headed north."

"But first, the butcher."

"What?"

"Then Loblaws."

She touches my arm, her hand very cold.

"Maybe we should stop in Drummondville after all," she says. "Get some rest. Didn't the Motel Couchant look nice?" Her other arm braces her belly like the baby might spill out.

There were no problems until the desk boy showed us our room. When he squinted at the trailer, I knew we should get out. Keep driving to Ontario. Or north, to the Arctic. But my love the engorged sun queen needed rest. The boy nodded at the parking lot, spoke in Franglais as thick as cheese curds: "*C'est comme le trailer* in *journal*, uh? I should *prendre un* look, *okie*?" I flapped my limbs at Blanche when he faced the other way, mouthed *Distract*. Then I stopped because I realized he was watching my shadow on the pavement.

She stared at me and shook her head, then turned to the concierge. "Show me how to work the coffee maker," she said. "I can never figure those things out."

They entered the room. I darted to the trailer—though when I got there, I hadn't a clue what to do. Maybe I could have enticed the tiger with a couple of T-bones. Pushed back the divider and lured her to the camels, forced them to respond more agreeably too. I could have herded my herd into the poorly pruned rhododendrons and waited for the desk boy to emerge from the room. But we never stopped at the butcher, and I didn't like the idea of that cat without bars. I only had time to lower each window blind before the boy jogged down the motel stairs.

"Yep, sold our stallions at the horse show today," I said, intercepting him at the curb. "Fix the coffee okay?"

He knew. I could tell by the way he smiled at me like I was waving a machete or driving a stolen trailer of zoo beasts.

"*Oui, bien*, yes," he said, and peered at the licence plate. "Okay, *d'accord*. Enjoy your stay, uh?" He grinned like that fucking camel and ducked into the office.

If we left then, the police would have been on our tails in minutes. So we stayed. I entered the room and found Blanche sitting very upright on the arm of a chair.

"Did he find them?" she asked.

"No."

She nodded and looked away. Then: "Someone should probably stay out in the trailer."

The camels communicate in throaty belches, both competing to hold their notes the longest, their eventual diminuendos reverberating through the floor into the arches of my feet. I found vitamins and a box of Medjool dates in a hideaway compartment behind the divider screen, which I removed in the interest of ventilation. I crouch atop that compartment now, the farthest distance I can manage from the dung. The beasts seem trained in that respect, or habitual, each favouring a particular corner, so the shit's not ubiquitous, just hilly. It stinks and it's cold, my toes clamming together in my open-air huaraches. But mostly my hair rises at how that giant cat poses so erect at the edge of his cage, yellow eyes on the door like he can will it open.

So the start sends me to my ass when she knocks. Soft and tinny, like she hopes I won't hear. Then she opens the door. It takes me a moment to realize she's carrying a pile of blankets—her silhouette grotesque and backlit by moon, an indefinable glob of pink, humanized only by the handbag off her shoulder, the tangle of blond adrift in the linen. The tiger stands at her entrance, rears his chin in a playful sort of way that is perverted by the bulk of his neck.

She walks to him, squats before the cage, and coos something sweet before turning to me. "It's chilly," she says, and releases the blankets.

I nod and tug a sheet from the pile, wrap it around my legs. She's changed into new clothes—jeans and a loose linen top. Cable-knit sweater tied around her waist.

"I was thinking," she says. "About Florida." She drapes a comforter over her shoulders and sits between me and the cage. Her nose flares in and out as it acclimatizes.

"About Ray-Anne," she says.

I know the day she means. Her pageant pal had stood at the door, smile as fake as her chest. *I'd invite you in, but I'm in the middle of sit-ups.* She had said her trainer kept her on a stern schedule and offered Blanche his card.

"Still a size two, still doing swimsuits," Blanche says. She lifts the hem of her top and folds it up her belly.

"I think you look exquisite."

She tightens the quilt over her shoulders, rises and pads to the cage. "That's what you said then too." She regards the tiger calmly and releases the latch.

A protest worms up my throat as she steps inside, but the tiger merely plows his cheek into the floor and rolls into a crescent. She kneels about a foot away. Traces with her finger the brassy glow that haloes his ears from the ceiling lights.

Tyger tyger, burning bright. In the forests of the night, we recline in the blue-collar *luxe* of polyester bedspreads. Miss Mississauga caged with the cat, and me alone on my perch. Left to dodge the swaying rumps and errant hoofs of camels. In her nest of pink linen, Blanche resumes the role of fertility goddess, legs bowed within the petals of a lotus. Her hair streams Rapunzeline down her shoulders, shrouds her chest. I'm entranced by her third eye. The blouse still rolled up, her belly the only stretch of flesh unsunned—it sits on her hips like a freshly domed igloo. As though every night for the last seven months, invisible children sleighed over her pelvis and added fistfuls more snow, packing the ice smooth with seal-mitted palms. Her navel's what stares me back. An imperfect O. Lips puckered for a kiss or a wish on a dandelion.

A camel grunts beside me and I feed him another date. His teeth are broader than I figured, and thick. I can smell the sugar off his tongue as he sucks the date from my fingers. I take one for myself. I press the dried fruit against the roof of my mouth until it dissolves into my gums. The overhead lamps shine on my queen elegiacally. Dust motes imprinting her shape onto the air like a projection, like if I switched off the light, her image would flicker into shadow. My love, the Queen of Central Ontario, embalmed by lamplight and in danger of blackout.

The RCMP and their special-suited animal handlers arrive before dawn. Each head for their respective beasts—the suits beelining for the camels and cage, a blue-shirted cop nudging my shoulder with her boot.

An hour or two earlier I pretended to sleep while Blanche phoned a cab from outside, her whispers muffled under a handkerchief or sweater sleeve. I watched from the hood of my bedsheet as she climbed back in, weaved through the trailer, stuffing sweater and loose belongings into her handbag, her footsteps heavy with the weight beneath her blouse. I shut my eyes and shrank deeper into my sheet as she padded toward me. Her belly sinking into my linen bedding, her lips pressing an O onto my cheek. She shut the door. The cat groaned from the cage. A car groaned from the parking lot.

M-I-S-S. But no, *je ne regrette rien.*

Sea Life

A woman marries young and quits her job as first AD for the TV series *Hellcats*. She purchases a teapot for the first time, and a cozy. Before marriage, she steeped her bags in a mug.

She begins a food blog and experiments with summer squash in her baking, like zucchini. She grates entire tubes of zucchini. Chocolate brownies, lavender tea loaf. *You'll never guess the secret ingredient.*

On warm mornings, she walks to the sea. She finds lilac and coral sea urchins. She holds her palm under the water to see how near she can reach to their spines.

~

She and her husband bought a home on the island four blocks from the beach. In the listing, the realtor had written sentences like *Holy Wow Factor! You must come & see. Popular Fairfield spot, ten minutes to Everything.* Their bedroom was on the second floor, with a skylight as long as the bed. The kitchen lay at the foot of the stairs, which facilitated her husband's fridge trips. He had a thing about milk. He trekked to the kitchen at 2 a.m. and imbibed entire pint mugs. The living room had been converted from a conservatory. The renovators kept the glass roof, and left the walls as full-length windows. *Two-hundred-seventy-degree view of garden and Garry oak tree.* She hadn't measured, but she suspected there was more window than wall space. From the street, the house looked like an aquarium.

One morning, her husband phoned to say he had invited a colleague for dinner on Friday. She had been in the living room, watching the girls next door play with a water hose. They looked eight, maybe nine years old, and wore sunken pink bikinis.

"She's a lesbian," her husband said, though she had missed why this was important.

Outside, the taller girl tried to drag their German short-haired pointer into the sprinkler. The small one darted behind and sprayed the dog's tail with a water pistol.

On the phone, her husband paused. She sensed that he sensed that she was not listening. She cleared her throat.

"I'll make beets," she said.

"What?"

She had seen a recipe that morning, on a cruise through other people's blogs.

"Beetroot gnocchi," she said.

"Okay ..." He paused again. This was not the answer to his question.

"Beetroot gnocchi in a cognac-and-thyme sauce," she said.

"Okay," he repeated. Then after a moment: "That sounds great."

Outside, the tall girl had yanked the dog right over the sprinkler. The small one stood away from them, her heels wide apart on the lawn. She clutched her water pistol and stared at the woman through the living room window. They made eye contact. She aimed the pistol at her and squeezed a stream of water onto the grass.

~

She could spend hours in a supermarket, even if she knew what she wanted. She liked to roll her cart down every aisle, between the bright plastics and foils, the cardboard boxes of cereal. She bypassed only Household Items. That day, she drove to the market after her husband called. She selected her beets, then fruit for the week—blueberries and nectarines, Gala apples, Ambrosias slipped in the bag with their stickers down. Next, she rolled her cart to the Bulk aisle. She shovelled jujubes and M&M's together, jostled the candy to hide the brown M&M's in the centre. Another bag for trail mix. One scoop of the cheap one with anonymous orange cubes. Two scoops California. A scoop of the cheap mix overtop. The macadamia nuts were priced $2.49 per hundred grams, so she released a few of those from the dispenser as well.

"Excuse me," said a voice. "Ma'am?"

An employee stood behind her with a trolley of yogurts, his arm extended in the air between them. She looked at his hand. He dropped it.

"You're not supposed to do that," he said. "You can't combine bulk items."

"Sorry," she said. "I didn't know."

He must have been seventeen, his hair combed over his eyes, chin tipped so he could see through his fringe.

"You need to separate them and label each one."

She looked at her bag. The macadamia nuts had sifted with the other two mixes. She couldn't distinguish which came from which.

"How?" she asked.

"With the scoop."

"But it's all blended," she said.

He bent toward the bag in her hand and prodded the plastic.

"Are there *three* mixes in there?"

"No," she said.

"I thought you only added the nuts."

She drew the bag away from him and cradled it in the nook of her elbow.

"I have to confiscate it, ma'am."

"Excuse me?"

"You can't take this bag to the till."

"But that's a waste."

"Please pass me the trail mix."

"Will you eat them?" she said.

"What?"

"Are you confiscating my dried fruit and nuts so that you may eat them?"

"Please pass me the bag."

"Because go ahead," she said. "But don't waste them."

She tossed him the bag, but he wasn't ready and it slid down his chest to the floor. She snatched it from the tile, delivered the mix into his hands, then marched her cart to the till.

Outside the supermarket, she rolled the trolley to their Buick, past the bike racks and sacks of manure, the grow-at-home mint and nasturtiums in cartons of soil. She loaded her groceries into the trunk and wheeled the cart to the metal snake at the store's entrance. When she returned to the car, she flicked the stereo volume knob to max, though the CD in the drive was Chopin's *Nocturnes*. She pulled from the parking space and listened to the nocturnes very loud. Something metal clattered into her trunk. She stamped the brake. Nothing appeared in the rear windshield. An SUV stopped behind her and a man in blue jeans leaped onto the pavement. An Asian woman sprinted from the crosswalk with her cart. It looked like the cart wrenched her forward. She felt nervous now. She felt the follicles on her forearms contract. She shut off the ignition and stepped from her car. A cluster of bananas sat ahead on the pavement, and next to that, an overturned flat of blueberries. As she wended around the trunk, she noticed the orange flag beneath her wheel. Then the miniature shopping cart, which had flipped upside down, her car's fender dipping into the wire basket. Under the cart, a girl lay nose down on the pavement. She wore a rubber jacket with rabbit ears stitched to the hood. The woman from the crosswalk shouted and together they yanked the cart from the fender, off the small girl, who did not cry. The Asian woman gathered the girl in her arms, and the blueberries that had pooled around her on the cement trickled into the storm drain. She herself stood with the cart dangling from her fist, her other hand clamped over her mouth.

The firemen arrived, then the ambulance. Lights raked from their trucks. The workers wore neon vests or jumpsuits, the police in darker uniforms. She found them easier to look at. A woman asked her questions while another photographed her tires. When they drove her home, their car idled in the driveway until she opened the front door. Inside, she watched them through the split in the blinds. She waited twenty seconds after the car pulled out before she walked to the bus stop.

At Emergency, she waited in the designated smoking area so the mother would not see her. She watched through the waiting room windows. The girl had been admitted. The mother sat outside the triage doors and stood every time a doctor passed.

Twice, a nurse joined her outside to smoke. The first time, she pretended she smoked too. She searched her pockets for cigarettes, though she knew she would not find any. She opened her purse.

"Leave yours inside?" he said.

"Yes."

"Here." He offered her his pack. She withdrew a cigarette and bent forward for him to light it.

An hour later, she leaned into the window with her forehead against the glass. When she stepped back to wipe the condensation, she saw his face in the pane, watching her. He tossed his butt to the curb and walked back inside.

In two hours and forty-three minutes, the mother changed her seat twice. She moved from the chair by the triage doors to the very back corner. Within five minutes, she returned to the chair by the triage doors. She had removed her blazer, but never set it down. She clutched it as she spoke to staff members. She shifted the jacket to one arm and dialed a number on her cellphone. Even through the window, she could see how her muscles tensed, how the fabric was clinched inside her elbow.

She wanted to buy the mother a coffee. She wanted to buy the mother one thousand coffees, and take her jacket and wait in the chair beside her and hold her hand. Or sit in her chair with the jacket and one thousand coffees to let the mother pee and stretch her legs. Instead, she watched through the glass and noticed every detail. Her hair looked hennaed. Wisps of it bulged from her head, as though that morning it had been pressed into a bun. She wore a high-waisted skirt with a back slit that had rotated to the side of her thigh. Her nude nylons were more tanned than her arms. Her arms were thin. She wore slingback heels.

No one joined her. Not her husband or mother or a neighbour with a foil-tented dinner and a pair of flat shoes. A nurse spoke with her. She could not read their lips or body language. The mother sat back down. Seventeen minutes after the first two hours and forty-three, nothing had changed. She had not brought a sweater. She could hear her forehead tremble into the glass. She wrapped her arms around her shoulders and crossed the parking lot. She jogged home this way—her hands locked to her biceps as though she wore a straitjacket.

At home in the living room, she cleaned the windows with vinegar and an old shirt. She had been watching the neighbours' yard when she noticed the streaks in the glass, noticed she could spell her name in them. Her husband had not returned yet from work. She thought he should have by then, though she hadn't phoned to say what happened. While she waited, she climbed onto the couch in bare feet and balanced on the tops of the cushions to reach the upper corners. The trouble with vinegar is that it does not clean windows. The streaks smudged no matter how hard she kneaded the rag into the glass. But she continued anyway, in case it dried clear. She knotted the shirt around her fist and swabbed the cloth with more vinegar. By the time her husband arrived, the pane was coated with milky spirals.

"You home?" he called when he opened the front door.

She heard him sling his coat on the rack in the hall. She stepped down to the lower cushions.

"Did you order fish and chips?" he asked as he walked in. When he saw the windows, he frowned.

"We're out of Windex," she said. Then her head felt inexplicably heavy, like it had been filled with stones. The length of her body thudded across the couch.

The girl had coasted on the back of her cart like a kick scooter. The woman did not see her because a Volvo had entered the adjacent space and obscured her view. The security tapes revealed this. The Volvo pulled in. The Buick backed out. The girl's cart rolled under her fender.

The woman sat in the sun on sharp grass. She had overdressed for the heat—her garden overalls and a plaid shirt, a hand towel draped over her head so the UV rays would not burn her. The warmth moored her hips to the lawn. It made her legs soupy; she knew she could not walk on them. So she sat, her wrists limp across her knees. She did not even go inside for a Kleenex. It irritated her when infants did this, when they did not sniff though a cord of mucus shone from their upper lip. Now she let herself leak too. She blew out a spume and felt the snot slink down her mouth. When she could not stand it, she wiped her nose with her shirt sleeve.

She had caught a cold last week, the week of the accident. The thinnest fluids had dried, but she still felt congested. "Flood it out," her husband said when he left that morning. "Lots of tea." But he would have questioned the two-litre bottle she brewed it in. She couldn't find their picnic Thermos, and coffee mugs weren't deep enough. So she used the Coke bottle and extra tea bags. She had selected five from different boxes: licorice; ginger-lemon; echinacea, which was a word she frequently misread. *Euthanasia*, the label read each time. Euthanasia tea. There were others. Hitler hi-liters. TO LET.

Next door, the German short-haired pointer had shucked its lead. She knew the breed, because her husband had commented when they moved in.

"Handsome pup," he had said.

"German short-haired pointer," said the guy-next-door, who later became the cardiologist-next-door, who later became the asshole-who-leaves-his-sprinkler-on-when-it's-raining.

"How old?"

"Eighteen months."

"So a year and a half."

"Yep," said the cardiologist. "Eighteen months."

Her husband had flown to Seattle that morning for work. He offered not to. He could have phoned "Clayton or Steve" to cover him, but she told him to go. She wanted a weekend alone. Now she sat on the wheatish grass that would cling to her poly/cotton overalls when she stood, and listened to the dog rattle the clematis on the other side of the fence. She could see his snout bobbing, and when he ducked his snout, his hay-coloured eyes. She scooted closer. She crouched opposite him and slipped her hand between two pickets. He sniffed her palm. He licked the space between her fingers.

At the end of the yard, the fence yielded to the Garry oak tree. A bough had sagged and split the wood, wedging enough space for a person to shimmy through. She whistled to the dog and tiptoed in that direction, dragging her fingernails along the planks. He swished after her on the other side. When they reached the tree, she clucked her tongue, and he thudded through the gap in the fence. He was a funny creature up close—his coat marbled like a horse, but brown as mud above the neck. The colour disembodied his head. And his ears were broad. He looked like he might tip over. He brushed past her toward the house. She stood and watched, unsure what to do. He trundled up the steps of her porch, sniffing the wood at each level. She had left the door open. He walked right in. She gathered her hand towel and tea and followed his path across the yard.

The hall was dim inside—she had not opened the drapes that morning. Once she closed the door behind her she could not see. As she walked through the living room, the lines of furniture crisped into shape. Light peeled through the slit between two blinds, the sun dust suspended like a third curtain. On the floor, the dog gnawed the leg of her wingback armchair. She continued her path into the kitchen.

She had not cooked a meal since the accident. They ordered in the first few days, and then her husband started barbecuing chickens. Entire birds, balanced on the grill with a beer can wedged up their rectum. It made her sick. He barbecued one last night, which sat in the fridge half-carved, its thighs still hugging a can of Pilsner. She lifted the plate from the shelf and pinched a slab of breast with her fingers.

"Hey, dog," she whispered, as she walked back through the French doors. He wasn't wearing a collar and she didn't know his name. "Hey, dog," she said again.

When he smelled the chicken, he barrelled for her, his tongue slack in his jaw like a wet sock. She guided him away from the carpet and tossed the meat on the floor. He licked it off. She pinched another strip.

She fell asleep. She did not mean to. Later, when she woke and wandered back into the living room, she found a bulge in the blinds, and the dog's docked tail trembling on the hardwood. He heard her footsteps and dashed out from the awning. He scampered down the hall to the back door. She tugged the cord and rolled the blinds up to her eye level. The cardiologist's SUV had not returned to the driveway, but she suspected it would by seven. It must be six now. Six thirty. The dog whined from the hall. She returned to the fridge and sliced some chicken into a Ziploc bag. She met the dog at the door and slipped into her leather sandals. He smelled the chicken off her fingers and barked. She hushed him. She opened the door. He bolted down the steps and across the yard. She whistled. She patted her knees, quietly so the neighbours would not hear her. She joined him at the fence and scratched his neck and fed him chicken. He licked her fingers. She lured him with her fingers down the road.

They walked to the sea. They followed the path she liked, to the rocks that rose from the sand at low tide. She liked this phase of summer, when the leaves bloated with so much green sun that the trees appeared to stoop. Oaks and alders cottoned from the beach and their dye seeped into the water. She picked her way across the rock, lunged over barnacles and mossy pools. The dog panted past her. He halted at the edge and backed himself around. He sniffed a crab shell. Beyond the reflection of trees, the water dimmed. It was a calm day. You could skip rocks. She crouched to her heels at a pool. The anemones slumped in the crevasses like seedy figs. They were green, mostly. Dark and loamy. Two starfish cleaved to the side of the rock, their legs aimed to her chin. She liked to find batches of them, their sodden limbs arced to a common point. She liked that the tide could mould them.

That night, she sat on her living room floor with a bowl of tea and a box of water biscuits. The dog lay beside her, the loose skin of his chin puddled between his paws. She broke a fragment off the biscuit and nibbled. The crumbs fell to her lap. She brushed them onto the floor. Every few minutes, she peeked behind the blinds to watch the cardiologist's headlights drift around the corner. He had circled the block three times. After the fourth lap, he parked the SUV on the boulevard, and the girls capered out of the car. They both carried flashlights. The tall girl sulked up the path to their door. The smaller girl shouted the dog's name. Beside her, the dog's ears pricked. He sat up. The cardiologist lifted the small girl onto his shoulders and shouted the dog's name also. The dog barked. She let the blinds drop. The dog skidded across the floor into the hall. He whined at the back door. She fetched the chicken from the fridge. He barked again. She rubbed his belly and scratched the dip between his shoulder blades. She fed him chicken.

She could not quite hear the name they called. It sounded like Oo-er. Maybe Cooper. Or Stewart.

"Cooper?" she said to the dog. She had set the chicken on the floor. He tongued the flesh off the carcass.

"Rupert?"

He clamped down on a drumstick. She tugged the bone from his jaw so that he would not choke.

Outside, she could no longer hear them. She padded back to the living room and pulled the string of the window blinds. She opened each one. It looked like the neighbours had gone to bed. Her only light shone from the lamp on the secretary. She bent down and yanked the cord. The room dipped into a sunken, nocturnal blue. She lay on the wood and let her limbs flop outward. She could sink there, in the deepwater light from the windows. She held her breath and let it submerge her.

~

The next morning she woke to the dog barking, the sun wedging through her eyelids. It sounded like the dog was outside, rapping the window. He barked when she didn't respond, then tapped again, lower on the glass, near her ear. Then he whimpered and pounded the upper window with his fist. She opened her eyes. Outside, the entire family stood on her deck. The cardiologist leaned into the pane with his wrist above his eyes to shade the sun. His wife, whom she had never seen, frowned beside him. She wore a hemp skirt. The small girl crouched between her heels with the skirt's hem hooded over her forehead. It was she who tapped the glass by her ear. The taller girl wore her mother's handbag over her shoulder. She needled the strap with her thumbs.

They looked like a portrait from a history textbook, taken before it was conventional to smile in photos. The dust bowl period. Stony-eyed peasants with their squints and long mouths, a bale of alfalfa behind them, a pitchfork.

She opened her eyes again. The cardiologist pounded on the window. She sat up. It took a moment to understand. When she did, her cheeks flushed. She pointed to the back door. She made a walking motion with her fingers. She pointed again to the back door. The family stared at her. She pulled herself off the floor and walked into the hall.

When she opened the door, the dog bounded past her onto the porch. The family picked their way across her lawn, and the dog greeted them. He barked and thrust his nose between their knees. The cardiologist stooped to clap the dog's flank.

The mother and the small girl continued to meet her on the porch. She stood with the door propped behind her.

"I'm sorry," she said, when they reached her. "I left the door open. He walked right in."

The mother didn't respond right away. She cupped her palms over her daughter's shoulders.

"I fell asleep," she added. "I hope you weren't too worried."

"He doesn't like his collar," said the mother. "If it happens again, could you phone us?"

"Of course. I should have phoned you."

"Do you have our number?"

"No."

The mother reached into her handbag, which she had reclaimed from her other daughter. She slid a business card from her wallet. The small girl stood between her legs and clutched a spear of Indian grass. She guided the spear over the door jamb, toward the woman's toes.

"That's Nate's cellphone," said the mother, indicating one of the numbers. "This is home."

The tip of the grass bumped over her big toe and grazed the outline of her foot. She and the girl both watched it. The grass felt nice. She wanted to laugh.

"Sophie, stop that." The mother pulled the little girl back into her hip.

"Oh, I don't mind," she said as she took the card. "Can I offer you tea?"

"Not now," said the mother. "Thank you."

"How about coffee? My husband bought this espresso machine. I've got biscotti in the freezer."

The girl arched away from her mother. She dangled the grass above her nose.

"Have you tried biscotti?" she asked the girl.

The girl shook her head, strands of hair catching her eyelashes.

"Well, this one is macadamia nut and apricot," she said. "It's dipped in white chocolate."

The girl plucked the hair tangled in her eyelashes and grinned into her palm.

"No, thank you," said the mother. "One of those weekends. You know how it is."

"Oh," she said. "I can imagine."

"Come on, Sophie."

The girl followed her mother down the steps. When they reached the lawn, she examined the woman one more time, purling her eyebrows together. The mother continued to the driveway. The girl skipped to catch up and the spear of grass drifted from her fingers.

The woman closed the back door. The chicken carcass sat on the floor beside her Wellingtons like a third, empty boot. She wondered if the mother saw. She found she did not care. She lifted the chicken by its scapula and walked to the kitchen. She tossed it in the trash.

The biscotti were folded in waxed paper, in a reindeer tin in the freezer. She pried off the lid and gnawed at a biscuit, though it was still frozen. The cookie cracked between her teeth, the white chocolate chipping like shards of teacups. She set the kettle on the stove. She ground the biscuit in her jaw. When the water boiled, she did not move the kettle, but leaned against the fridge and listened to it. She tried to match the whistle with a whine from the roof of the mouth. This ached her palate, but she found she could harmonize. Like how you do with humpbacks. The kettle wailed and she harmonized, but the achy feeling didn't fall away.

Thoughts, Hints, and Anecdotes Concerning Points of Taste and the Art of Making One's Self Agreeable: A Handbook for Ladies

FASHION AND DRESS

The plainest dress is always the most genteel. Ladies with pale pigments should abstain from palettes of undue intensity. Never wear coloured gloves. Never wear jewellery before noon. Embrace lace. If you've a gangly neck, moderate exaggeration of the collar reduces the appearance of awkwardness.

Tonight I don't care. My sister-in-law's black and white Thanksgiving ball: I wear red instead. Scarlet moiré and rubied bust, a dyed ostrich plume in my hair.

My husband's mouth is knotted. He weaves me through murmurs, gawks, glimmers of smiles, his fingers cold and clenched on my elbow.

"Exhibitionist," he says, as I place my hand on his shoulder for a dance.

We waltz one, two, three, and soak their stares like pickled lemon. He spins me in hard circles, so I clutch his shoulder tighter and arch my heart to the chandelier. When the violins dwindle, his nails still dig into the palm of my glove. He tells me to retrieve my cloak. Instead, I smile luminously at his colleague from the bank. The colleague bows. His lady averts her eyes. I twist my wrist from my husband's grasp and lift my gown and curtsy. I say, "How do you do?" because it is poor taste for married women to pose such inquiries at unfamiliar men.

"Very well," says the colleague.

"An arresting gown," says his wife.

"And yours," I reply, "is so very columnar."

My husband hisses in my ear.

"Now, now, my pet," I say, and paw the breast of his waistcoat. The threads rip when he reels for the door, his satin pocket dangling from my fingers.

AGREEABILITY OF SUBMISSION IN PRIVATE DISPUTE

He locked me out. So I warm my lips with rum from a flask and recline beneath the gargoyle in my opera cape. I watch the horses trot mutely over snow. Watch the lamplighter fill lanterns with oil. Watch the snow melt into my shoe until the suede turns glossy. I can count the years of my marriage like rings of a tree. Year one, a snapped rib; year two, fractured jaw. The day after tomorrow, year five. At least we've no children. They can't be mended like bones; can't be rolled in plaster, shrouded under furs.

My toes have frozen together. I try to separate them inside my shoe. On the lowest rail of the porch, there is a crow. Happy Thanksgiving, crow. Tonight I forgot to give thanks. So: thanks. For my cape and the wolf that trims my hood. For the rum. Thanks especially for the rum. Ingratitude is so unappealing in a wife.

I topple inside when the front door opens. My heels land apart on the porch, my skull flat on the oriental rug in the hall. I see the hydrangeas drying on the wall behind me, then Bernard's face, upside down.

"Madam, I couldn't let you in until Mr. Irvine retired."

He looks concerned.

"I've drawn a bath," he says. "Your lips are blue."

"I'll take a hot toddy in the scullery," I say. "And fetch me Mr. Irvine's waistcoat."

ON MENDING

A stitch in time saves nine. Keep a cushion with threaded needles at the end of your ironing board to complete the mending and pressing at once. To repair a pocket, hold the edges in place with adhesive tape rather than pins. Stitch through the tape and peel it off once you've finished. When you iron the garment, press a spoon over each button so the buttons do not melt.

The needle doesn't puncture as smoothly as I'd like. The point wriggles through the satin, puckers the weave. *Once around the back*, my fingers still fuchsia with cold. *In through the front door*. Almost. I twist the needle deeper. There. In through the front, again around the back. This time I stab. The needle pierces the tape, glides through the fabric, but the other side's blocked, like I'm sewing through cork. Where my left hand holds the reverse side, the thread is sticky. I open the vest. Three tidy stitches link the satin to the pad of my index finger. The blood is thin and florid.

CARRIAGE OF A WIFE

To keep a happy home is the office of a woman. Her elegance is paramount to domestic stability. Vexed will be the husband who returns to find the house in disorder and his wife *en déshabille*. When domestic storms brew, only a meek, blithesome disposition will shelter you from the rain. Learn to keep silence even if you know your husband to be wrong. The stoutest armour is a cordial spirit (and spirit in the glass doesn't hurt).

I wear a mint-green dress with silk cuffs and buttons the size of thumbtacks. My stockings are grey wool, the heels of my shoes sensible and low, and my palm balances a tumbler of Scotch.

I say, "Ice, darling?"

He wears a tweed vest and trousers that sit fashionably above the ankle. His socks are brown wool, he reads the newspaper, and his fingers clasp a cigarette.

"You know I drink whisky neat."

"Tomorrow I'll take your waistcoat to the tailor's."

He says nothing.

"He'll mend the pocket," I say, but his eyes never waver from the page.

"I tried to mend it myself last night, but silly me I pricked my finger."

I set his Scotch on the lamp table beside his elbow and sit in the opposite chair. "Serves me right for sewing without a thimble."

He stares over the brim of his glasses at the newspaper.

"They say a woman is fundamentally selfish until she has children."

He turns the page.

"How silly." I press a pleat that jets from my waist to the dress's hem.

"And we've tried."

"Not very hard," he says.

I allow my mouth to twitch.

"Indeed."

"We sleep separately."

"You hate children."

"People pose questions."

Bernard slides through the double doors with a tray, which holds an open velvet box and a sherry glass.

"I'd like you to see someone about your fertility," my husband continues.

Bernard lowers the tray to me. A diamond paste choker lies balled in the corner of the box. I pinch an edge of the choker and drape it against my knee. I swipe the sherry glass next and spill the liquid to the back of my throat. When I dangle the glass above my lip, it looks like a church bell.

HINTS ON FECUNDITY

Warm the womb. Draw a bath prior to intercourse or drape a tepid cloth over your pelvic area.

Simmer two teaspoons of snakeroot in one pint of water. Swallow three tablespoons of the tea six times a day.

In four quarts of water, boil seventy chrysanthemums. Steep twenty minutes, strain, and serve with honey.

Massage belly with mint oil.

I feel love in the backs of my eyes. A warmth that tickles my retinas like goose feathers slid under my eyelids, that raises the hairs from my forearms. It blooms a grin from my throat before I can think to smile. I feel love when his chin dimples. When the pulse of his wrist beats hot and gentle against my chest.

STAINS: TIPS AND CLUES

For bloodstains it's either molasses or peppermint oil. I try molasses first. I spoon it onto his waistcoat in the shape of a heart. For good luck I try peppermint too. But then I worry the oil will leave a stain. I know the quickest grease reliever is melted wax, so I light a candle from the tree.

I'm dripping wax pearls along the left ventricle of my molasses, when I see him in the door frame. His lips are sucked in, his cheeks pointy, and a lilac vein worms up his neck from his collar. When he throws his briefcase, I duck behind the butcher block, and it lands on the counter behind me, on the fruit bowl. The figs sail plummy arcs above our heads and land with bruised plops on the floor. I stay crouched. As I breathe, my back knocks the cupboard door. His soles clack along the linoleum. I look to see him above me with the candle. He steps forward onto a fig, then drops or throws the candlestick. The brass clangs onto the floor. When he stalks from the room, the fig is still suctioned to his heel.

STAINS: TIPS AND CLUES (CONT'D)

To wipe burns from linoleum, rub steel wool in the direction of the grain. Soak your garments in buttermilk to remove fruit stains. Clean the white rings from water glasses &c with a paste of cigarette ash and vegetable oil. Paint the paste onto the mark, let stand thirty minutes, then rub with a wet cloth. Shrink the puffy patches beneath your eyes with lightly beaten egg white. Let dry and rinse.

KITCHENS AND COOKERY

His mother cooked his father figgy pudding. She shelled her own hazelnuts, grated her own nutmeg. She steeped dried currants in brandy, beat yolks into custard. She knew that butter the size of an egg was four tablespoons.

To thicken cream, cover your bowl with a muslin cloth and leave overnight. Heat milk with a pinch of bicarbonate to prevent curdling. An apple in your brown sugar keeps the sugar moist. A bay leaf in your flour keeps the flour dry. Store nutmeg away from children. Ingestion in excess of one seed can cause hallucinations and stop the heart.

Combine in a bowl, one cup sultanas and half that red currants, steamed figs, and pitted dates. Pour in half a mickey of brandy. Soak six hours, or until the fruit glistens and the sultanas bloat into waterlogged toes. In a different bowl, cream brown sugar, two eggs, and four eggs of butter. Add buttermilk. Then shell your hazelnuts. Grind them with pestle and pour over fruit. Add flour. Add sodium bicarbonate. Add wet ingredients and a spoonful of cinnamon. Stir mixture well. Pour into a Bundt pan. Bake sixty minutes.

A husband can gauge his wife's temper by the quality of her cooking. Foul moods are betrayed by too much spice, by the sour lumps of baking powder in her scones. Conversely, a wife's sweetness raises the height of her soufflé, harmonizes the nutmeg and cloves in her buttered rum.

ON FLOWERS

A dining table without a floral arrangement is Paris without the Eiffel Tower. Is a petticoat without the gown. Is a peacock with crow feathers. Don't: combine multiple colour schemes, add greenery as filler. Do: snip the stems on a slant, sweeten the water with sugar cubes, match flowers to season. Only work with odd numbers of stems and ensure the height of your bouquet is three times the width.

I choose snowberries over poinsettias because poinsettias are too easy. Because as a girl I wound a branch of the former into a crown and coronated myself snow queen. Because when I press the berries under water, they spit bubbles like baby lips.

SPIRITS, &C

On Thursdays my husband drinks whisky with colleagues at the Astor House, and our anniversary is no exception. He will arrive home late with spider-legged eyes and require a buttered rum *tout de suite*. A ready wife plans ahead, works ahead. Softens the butter. Measures the rum. Grates the nutmeg.

I haven't eaten because it's Bernard's day off. Because a wife must watch her hips, particularly if she expects to be expectant. The four nutmeg seeds sit taut as knuckles on the saucer. Their outer crusts snaked with hairy ridges, though smooth between my fingers. I stroke a seed slowly down the grater until I have whittled it in half. Then I clean the underside. I slide my fingers down the grater and collect the shavings on my thumb.

The second nutmeg grates as easy, blooms through the eyelets in oily flakes. Then the third seed, and the fourth. I rub the last in quick strokes, grate it to nothing. Past nothing, and this time I feel it sting. Five red lines carve my thumb and seep together. Serves me right for cooking without a thimble.

The trick is to melt enough butter and brown sugar to temper four seeds of nutmeg. It forms a thick sludge. I add water. I add a cinnamon stick and a pinch of dried cloves. I let it simmer for four hours, or until my husband returns for a fifth anniversary peck on the cheek and an after-cocktail cocktail.

THE LADY'S TOILET

I choose a lilac gown to bring out the blue in my bosom. The lace collar mollifies my neck. I hold my face in a hand-held mirror: my cheeks lightened by powdered lead, my curls wound taut from pins. My girlhood doll sits beside me at the vanity. I paint my mouth like hers, into a cupid's bow. Then I rub my palms with almond oil. Last step is nightshade. A drop of nightshade in each eye will dilate the pupils to illuminate my gaze.

FEMININE TOILS

I wait for him in the kitchen. The butcher block is still lumped with flour from the morning's baking, but I lie on it, on my stomach, grey satin pumps dangling off my heels. I wipe the flour into the corner of the block, into a soft mound. I dip my hand in it. The backs of my fingers. I wear the powder like a glove. Never put on gloves in public. Never remove them for handshakes or dancing or kisses on the back of your wrist. As a girl I wrote a code: Lay a glove on your lap to ask for an introduction. Drag it around your ear to request a dance. Drop the left to say I Love You. Drop both to say We're Being Watched.

When the front door opens, I hear the wind tumble in,

and the rustle of the hydrangeas in the hall, the springs of his armchair as he sits.

"Darling?" he calls.

I fetch the rum from the cabinet and pour it all in the pot. I bring the liquid to a gentle boil. There isn't a glass large enough to contain it all, but three-quarters fit into a beer stein. I garnish with a cinnamon stick and glide through the sitting room doors.

His pelvis is thrust to the edge of the seat cushion, and he's trying to remove his shoe.

"Darling," he repeats.

"Happy Anniversary," I say, and cross the salon to kneel by his chair. "I've cooked you a buttered rum."

"How charming," he says. Then: "It's gargantuan."

"I considered a smaller glass, but realized it must be particularly cold outside." I tug the shoe from his foot. "Given the colour of your nose."

He grabs the stein and tips it into his mouth. He lurches forward as if to gag, squeezes his lips together and swallows.

"It's repulsive." He peers into the mug. "What rum did you use?"

"Spiced."

He swirls the liquid. "The bottle from the Jeffreys?"

"Oh, yes."

"From the Indies?"

"That's right. It's very fine."

"It's vile."

"And so fashionable."

He swallows another gulp and winces. "How much sugar is in here?"

"I know your sweet tooth."

"Darling," he says.

"Yes?"

"Your hand is covered with powder."

I slip off his second shoe, the heel still stained from the fig.

He sips again. "I think it's growing on me." He raises the stein. "Here's to the mud in your eye."

ON SERVING DESSERT

Five hours post-rum, recumbent in bed and drifting between dreams, cocooned under layers of candy-striped eiderdown, legs butterflied, knees pointed out, the hot water pig clamped between the soles of my feet, I remember the figgy pudding. I go downstairs, where I had left it on the kitchen counter to cool. I loosen the dough from the Bundt pan and plop it onto a plate. We're out of rum, so I pour brandy on the top. Upstairs, I strike a match and light it. My husband does not answer when I say his name, but his door is unlocked. The bed is tousled and empty, and there are wheezes from the bathroom. He's on the tile. I see him in flashes, by the blue flames that flutter over my pudding. His body is wedged between the radiator and bathtub, and his eyes have rolled so far into their sockets they quiver. His tongue is raw and fat, slumping out of his jaw. He grunts with my entrance, rocks his body to the side, chipping the paint on the tub with his teeth. The fire shrinks as I draw the plate over his body, his shins crumpled through the loops of the radiator, his big toe flapping against the wall.

FOR THE EXPECTANT MOTHER

I paper the walls of his room with white cranes. Then I make a mobile. I fold foil into stars and string them to the canopy with floss—flat tin suns to dangle above her chin. I crochet bonnets and booties: white wool for newborns, cerise and pale green after six months. I collect pussy willows in champagne bottles and keep them on the floor. I like mazes, like to wind through green glass and down-tipped branches in order to reach my window.

She will adopt my doll. Bisque cheeks and mohair curls, cotton torso stuffed with straw. I stitch silk ribbon to the hem of Dainty Dorothy's crinoline and patch the chips on her mouth with paint. If my daughter wants curls like hers, I will show her how to roll her hair in pins. How to sew ribbons. How to tint her lips with cupid bows and how not to let them crack.

Good for the Bones

Sharing the window seat with a gentleman and nothing under her nightgown. Adele doesn't notice him until now. He's got a few years on her—skin everywhere the same iridescent pink. New, fresh-out-of-the-womb luminous like an albino, like if her finger grazed his cheek it would break out in rash. The girl perches across from them on the windowsill. She's young, red hair. Every time she leans over the food tray her braid dips into the bottom of Adele's fruit cup. A small pot of yogurt sits on the tray too. It is unclear to her whether it is breakfast or lunch.

"Uncle Rog?" the girl says. "Yogurt?" She ticks the plastic container back and forth. The man shakes his head.

The yogurt is a sickly flavour at room temperature. Good for the bones, the girl says, but what are her bones good for? Sitting, folding neat like a hand-held fan. Good bones rich in calcium and phosphorus, fine for planting bulbs. With hers she would like to grow snowdrops. Commit her body to the ground—earth to earth, ashes to ashes, dust to dirt to February blooms. A cheering sight for the winter weary.

A man sits next to her at the window. Her thighs and kneecaps look bare and she can't think where in this room she keeps her pantyhose. She can feel something against her neck. It scratches every time she moves her head, so she leans forward and asks if the man can see. His fingers warm the base of her hairline. It feels like he is untying a string.

"There," he says.

She sits up and a vinyl bib drifts down her chest.

She's perhaps at one of her agent's retreats. A centre for healing, for rehabilitation and excavating the nostrils. Never checked herself in, but had she ever? Outside her window, a man-made pond: telltale sign. The pump burbling in the centre like a plastic sphincter in a tub with nothing to hide. Next to the pond, a cherry tree with bronchiole branches, and under the tree an uncomfortable-looking bench. The man beside her wears terry-cloth slippers fit for kicking buckets. Patches of brown on the heels, and he himself positively macabre. Skin like pink sidewalk chalk—aglow in the way of transparent spiders *sous terre*.

"Hey, mister, got a cig?" she says, and his pale stare locks with hers.

"Oh, Addie. No."

Those cryogenic eyes red rimmed now. Veins sucking the whites, suction cup safety harnesses to keep the balls in their sockets. She finds her feet below her, clutches the chair arm, struggles toward up. Clenches thighs for momentum, but falls back into the cushion.

"Auntie, are you okay?"

The girl with ginger hair sprints from the doorway. She wears a white shirtwaister and tennis shoes—can't be over eighteen.

"It's Addie," says Adele as she glances at the man. "Just weak on my feet."

"Do you need to use the bathroom?" The girl beside her now, clutching her elbows, hoisting her up.

"I beg your pardon," says Adele as she palms the hem of her nightie. She squeezes between girl and recliner, and every second coagulates as she lurches for the door. "Just powdering my nose," she adds. Rehab pun to save face.

~

Her tongue steeped in lime Jell-O. Grand window-side vista confined to a dreary tree and bargain-bin pond; DIY-Susie-Homemaker, no doubt: connect part X (the pump) to part Y (the hose) into part Z (a hole). The tube in the centre of the pond bubbles off and on, then off for good. The windowpanes are smeared with cleaning streaks and nose prints, and superimposed over that is the reflection of an old man's face. The corners of his mouth are stained red. Adele glances right. "They got you with cherry?"

~

Swell party last night. Three too many Singapore Slings, but what's a Sunday without a migraine? The fossil beside her awake but with eyes closed, tucked inside a flannel housecoat, in slippers a dog wouldn't chew, his calves blanched and reflecting the sunlight that pours from the window. Too old to bother drying out, but to each his own.

"Tabitha Tate's a veritable gargoyle," she says. "But she throws the most sensational parties. Frankie Carle stroking those keys, "Little Jack Frost Get Lost," and I won second in the Charleston contest. First place was sure as rain mine, but Emmie found Stell Gray and the Louisiana judge dancing the back-seat mambo before third round, so she was a sure win. And that man from Atlantic City, Mr. Roger Foss, his toes butter at first, but by nine a regular Gene Kelly. His eyes positively cerulean. By one the rains started, and you know L.A., a month's downpour in a single day. I told Mr. Foss that nothing invigorates me like a Los Angeles monsoon, so by 1:15 we were lindy-hopping the puddles up Wilshire. We found the finest pools at the bases of driveways, and it became a game—the *stompeur* of the highest vertical splash earned a wish, but neither of us consented to spell our wishes aloud, so when I broke the eleven–eleven tie at 2:30, I asked for a cuppa joe at Ruby's."

Adele glances again at the old man, him sitting stone still, eyelids squeezed shut as if intent on pretending to sleep.

"And that's where we stayed till five," she says. "Ruby's Diner." Her retinas pound, so she rests her eyes on the window. Last night a few too many Singapore Slings.

Smoking a Winston with an orderly on the balcony. Nowadays most girls buy Slims, but it's real class to smoke men's cigs like a lady. First rule's to keep your fingers on the filter to make the cigarettes look longer. Always draw the filter to the centre of your lips, never the sides, and be certain to frame your cheek with a skyward-pointed forearm. A lady never lights her own cigarette, and a proper gentleman won't need a reminder.

"You're withering your lungs."

The red-headed girl slides the door closed with her hip. She must be a nurse. Each day the bags under her eyes look a little more like plums.

"Darling, I hope they pay you overtime," says Adele.

The girl steadies her gaze on the balcony rails.

Adele stares at the orderly. "Well, aren't you going to offer her a cigarette?"

Nineteen fifty-nine and six weeks after her mastectomy, Adele lay in bed and examined the wallpaper, the violet yellowing on patches afflicted by sun. Beside her on the nightstand: a bouquet of ginger lilies *From Donnie with Love, you're still tops kid,* XOXO. The lilies two weeks old and overwatered, petals furling, rusting, limp. Roger had entered with his tray, set it on the dresser, opened the blinds. She told him the sun was pulverizing her wallpaper, but he continued to crank the string, said she needed the vitamin D. He brought the tray to her lap—poached eggs on toast, sliced orange, four Demerol, and a copita of sherry. She slid her palm under the plate and flung it at the wall. The plate sank to the floor unbroken, the anticlimax unbearable, yolks cracked though, sunny-side smears dribbling down sunbathed wallpaper, the toast butter-side down on the hardwood. Roger peeled the plate from the floor. His patience rancorous. She gathered the pills, laid them one by one on her tongue, ants on a log till she tasted the sour, then washed them back with the sherry.

While Roger fetched a cloth, Adele had sat at the edge of her bed, and drew circles on the floor with her pointed toe, foot cramping, then flexing, then falling still on the oak. Her waves wilted like the lilies, webbed over her shoulder blades, sticky with sweat. Gumboot summers at Grandmother's lagoon on the Oregon coast, uprooting boulders: thumb-nail-sized crabs scattering like pool balls, now in her breast, her un-breast, nerves scrambling, repairing, and searching for phantom links, for broken ends. She lifted the gown over her head. The flesh on her left pectoral folded neatly and stitched like a muted mouth. The cave of her breast cycloptic. Flat and white and gone. Roger came in a few minutes later with his cloth, lips agape at first, then clasped shut. He hadn't seen since the bandage removal. Him beside her then, stroking her shoulder, brushing hair back, his palms warm like worn leather. Adele watched through wet lashes. His palm hovered above the hollow of her breast, then sank. Fingers a fist to fill the gorge, hermit crab to a perfect-sized shell.

~

On her lap, a chartreuse stain the shape of a tadpole. She reaches into her nightgown pocket for a handkerchief and her fist re-emerges with a tangle of hair. A whoop from her throat—first thought Señor Lemon, her brother's pearly furred rabbit from the fifth grade, the hair in her palm just as white but too long, knotted around her fingers, looped between knuckles. A bulge in her other pocket too. Her pinky hovers at the lip, then hooks inside. More hair. Her hands spring out and the hairs cast off her palms. Strands wafting, settling inside the collar of her nightgown, on her lap, on the sea-foam carpet in between her toes. She lifts her hand to her head, scalp nude save a few curls, pinches a lock and tugs, the tuft freeing without a moment's deliberation, now slipping through her fingers. The man in the recliner beside her watches and waits with a calm she could cling to.

Except she has garnet waves to make Rita Hayworth green, as thick and amber as treacle. Another tug, another tuft. She glances at the man. "Will you help?"

She shuffles her sit bones back and forth on the cushion until her knees point in his direction, folds collarbone to thigh, forehead to knee, her nape toward the ceiling. Her fingers roam the ridges of her skull, tugging, yanking, and his hands navigate too, palm pads warm and tugging more gently—white hairs swirling like feathers in a cockfight, like a freshly gutted pillow.

~

The room's empty save a geriatric with eyes like her ex-husband's. He leans against the window with a cinnamon roll, next to a newspaper and grease-glossed paper bag.

"You missed Cait," he says, thumbs deep in bun. "She stopped at the patisserie." Butter congealed beneath his cuticles, cinnamon in the corners of his mouth. "Cinnamon roll?"

Adele lies in one of the two twin beds. "No, thanks."

He sets down the bun and wipes his fingers on the newspaper. President Obama—no Soviets, no Nixon—and he's bedside now, loosening the sheets with his thumb, knee on the mattress. He deflates beside her, places his palm on her cheek, then sweeps past her ear, his skin on hers, her scalp. Phantom hairs as pathologically hopeful as phantom breasts.

"My husband and I owned a *casa* on Telegraph Hill," she says. "Small—one thousand square feet, low ceilings. But with a kitchen skylight fifteen feet high and right in the centre of the house. Death trap for bees, the poor things. Fat with pollen and spiralling for cloud, only to hit glass and find themselves incapable of flying down. So they'd buzz up there for days."

She rests her chin on his shoulder, then continues. "We couldn't help," she says. "The skylight too high and welded shut." His palm sinks back to her cheek. His fingertips are sticky. They smell of cinnamon. His index finger traces her lip, his nail shaping letters. Words like abbreviations across her mouth, like signals from a cable under water.

Here Be Dragons

LISBON

At the café on Rua Garrett, you are the woman who serves me sardines. I sit under a yolk-gold umbrella. She threads through tables pelvis first, answers queries on wine: From the Minho region, No, the colour is not green, In Portuguese we pronounce it *verde*. Like yours, her eyes are the India-ink spills labelled as islands by our forebears. And her hair. Her hair defies neatlines. Had I known this spot was so hot for tourists, for burned-cheeked Britons and McAmericans, university gals with backpacks and Birkenstocks, their boyfriends with Hacky Sacks and ponytails, had I known this I'd have ordered my fish from a hole-in-the-whitewashed-wall of Miradouro de Santa Luzia. But then I'd have missed you. Like you she wears black curls thick enough to catch bees. Faded jeans—high waist, wide hips—and a sea-green top that clings to the contours of her Northern Hemisphere. But what really grabs me, what really clutches me by the collar and flashes me back, is how she hangs behind the bar between orders. Pregnant gulps from an under-the-counter *pintada*, then back at my table, lips wet with foam. The extent of your career as a waitress may be merCator, but you punctuated your work just the same.

To my left, a Tampa Bay fan with a blond mullet pretends to be Canadian: I'm from the capital, you know, Toronto, you know. East of me, a woman from Toronto pretends to be Canadian: So the ferries to Vancouver went on strike. So why didn't you just drive? I want to tell you and Our Lady of the Immaculate Tables that I'm not like them. I'm here on business. To ink lines on paper, call them roads, to graph cities over grids. To define place. Instead, I say, Portuguese sardines are bigger than the ones back home. Truly, its spine stretches across my plate like a rat's tail. Our Lady of the Immaculate Tables looks beyond me and asks if I'll order another *cerveja*.

At Ribeira Market, I buy a pear and a bag of pine nuts, then hop the number 28 tram. Lisbon, like Rome, is a city built on seven hills. But the Portuguese carved tracks into their cobblestones, fit the tracks with aluminum shoeboxes, wide windowed and painted sunny, to chug pedestrians up the narrow walled slopes. On the 28 you are the Portuguese mother of two, breastfeeding one and scolding the second for peeling gum off the seat. This time it's the way she is not ashamed. To breastfeed, to sculpt *P*'s with spit (*P-or favor*), to wear her brows thick and a shadow above the lip. I like that you never used bleach.

Girl of the Seat Gum can't be older than six. Her hair is tied with a dark green scarf, the boiled-spinach shade of lower elevations, and her forehead is bridged with a symmetrically pristine unibrow. I offer Girl of the Seat Gum a handful of pine nuts and she looks to her mother, who nods and switches breasts.

You who met your zenith before we had children to peel gum off seats. You who died On Business, K.I.A.: calves plush with rash and a forehead I could sauté garlic on. Pro bono land survey for the new primary school in Arusha, and we popped enough Lariam to dream Technicolor for a month. But there's no fix for dengue, the breakbone, no Preventative Measures beyond long sleeves and repellent. You who hated repellent, the smell of science-pickled eyeballs, the way it made your fingers sticky and how you could taste it in your morning *chapatti*. K.I.A., but That Was Africa. Shit happens, *hakuna matata*. You always as crazy cool as bananas in the refrigerator. You, the centre of my celestial sphere.

The tram inches between walls with wash lines that hang skirts and neon bras like prayer flags. I disembark on Calçada do Combro and walk from here to the Miradouro de Santa Catarina. The mother and daughter get off at the same stop and walk a few paces ahead of me. Lisbon's *miradouros* and funiculars remind me of Grouse Mountain, except these trams run on tracks, and instead of evergreens there are white box buildings, and instead of you fingering our initials into breath on the window, there's Our Mother of the Ample Bosom forbidding her daughter to throw pine nuts at pigeons. As I near the lookout, I see an oval lawn and the statue of the Adamastor. Spirit of the Cape, Gatekeeper of the Indian Ocean, "heavy jowls, and an unkempt beard / Scowling from shrunken, hollow eyes / ... mouth coal black, teeth yellow with decay." I taunt the Adamastor with nuts. I stretch my sardine fingers toward the stony bulges of his facial hair. I say, Come and Get Me. Four shirtless men sit on the wall that encloses the lawn, and when I turn from the monster, they're staring and one of them hucks a can.

At the Church of Our Lady Queen of Martyrs, you are the nun with gap teeth and two-toned eyes. Heterochromia, she says. One yellow, one brown. Two-Toned carries wood sorrel with both hands like it's a snake and leads me down white brick steps to the courtyard. She tosses the sorrel into the disputed hedge of the neighbouring vineyard, and I set up the tripod for my theodolite. Hired by God this round, or at least one of His Portuguese ambassadors, to define the property lines between church and grape—A matter to be settled post-haste, said the abbot over the telephone: they've cut off the free wine.

The machine is two silver panels on either side of a lens, and when I'm feeling congenial, I call it my Cyclops. I centre my *x* on God and grapes' distant wall and align my *y* with local gravity. I am Lee Harvey Oswald because my eyes blink through crosshairs. Because *triangulate* sounds so violent.

Two-Toned wears a grey veil and no habit. Rosary beads hook from the belt loops of her jeans, and as she walks, a wooden cross bounces against her hip. You become her when she stands beside a shrub to collect quinces with a priest's black biretta. She sings Nancy Sinatra and balances the fruit in the hat, the quinces yellow and knobbed like cancerous lemons. And then there's you in the valley gathering cherries in the belly of your May The Forks Be With You apron, humming something bluesy that neither of us knows the name of.

Two-Toned sees I'm watching her instead of the theodolite and tosses me a quince.

You know how to play with *marmelos*? she says.

I answer, How?

It's a game for the sea, a group game, catch and swim. *Marmelos* are sour, but sweet with salt water. So the first person pitches and everyone swims, and whoever fetches the *marmelo* first takes a bite and pitches again, and everyone swims, over and over till it's eaten.

Catch the Quince, I say, how charming. And to think back home we're stuck spinning bottles.

You have *esposa*? she replies. A wife?

I say, Oh. I say, Not yet, but I'm engaged.

After my romp with Pythagoras in the crosshairs I want the Bigger Picture, the three-sixty, so Two-Toned leads me back up the helix of white bricks to the church's roof, to the panoramic view. The wall up here is painted blue on white ceramic tiles. It's a sea mural, bordered by vases and ropes of flowers and pillars that rest on the plump shoulders of cherubs. In the scene, azure women arch from arcs of azure spray, and waves swell over a cliff until my eyes adjust and I realize the waves are the manes of rearing horses.

Two-Toned sits now before a bench stacked with faded tiles and fist-sized jars of paint. I restore *azulejos*, she says, and dabs a blue-slicked brush into the shadow of what might be a cherub's belly button.

Of course you do, I say. My fiancée restored maps.

I step onto the strip of clay tiles that borders the roof's edge. I see vineyards and pear trees, plump jade acres that are eventually flattened by the bleached walls of a nearby township. I wager with myself the distance between that steeple and that chimney, and that chimney and me, and me and the ground, and I add up my angles: the angles it takes to join the one-eighty. To leap off the roof into the y axis. To bisect my horizon.

ST. PETERSBURG

Palace Square at 4:45 in the ante meridiem inspires me to re-instate the tsar. A city of four and a half million people and I stand with my Cyclops in a forty-thousand-square-metre expanse of silence. The facade parabolas across the square, and I am the focus point to its vertex. The lonely guy in a beaver pelt *ushanka* opposite Triumphal Arch. My assignment: to collect data for a three-dimensional three-sixty online interactive tour map to end all tour maps.

It occurs to me that I'm listening to a series of chinks, and a shoulder check reveals a heavy-coated security guard in a navy blue saucer cap, leaning against the base of the Alexander Column. He's clipping his fingernails. A grey sliver zings toward me.

A good one, he says, and I don't know if he means the shot or the nail. The blades chime together again and a clipping drops onto his shoe. I say, *Privet*, and try to recall if it translates to hello or thanks or toilet. *Privet*, he says. I tell him I'm here to collect data. You are map man, he says. *Da*,

I reply, I am Map Man. He peers through the wrong side of my Cycloptic lens and says, Eet's hard? I say, Easier than it looks, and he replies, *Da, da*, the casket open in simple way. He tells me inside is warmer and asks if I like art. So I bag One-Eye, collapse the tripod, and follow him into the far left entrance.

In the Winter Palace you are Elizabeth Petrovna in *Portrait of Elizabeth Petrovna on Horseback Accompanied by a Negro Servant*. The painting hangs at the end of a gilded hall: velvet carpet, vaulted ceilings, pillars that drip gold leaf and angel hair. You're jaunty in a tricorn hat and riding coat, avocado green, wide cuffs, white gloves. Tall-piped boots that end above the knee, a length disproportionate to the foot on the stirrup. The mare's tail flows like it's been brushed in the mirror one hundred strokes a day, and the Negro Servant is clad like a *petit prince*: white tights, pink sash, gold-braid blouse. Far cry from the Maasai warrior who led our camel in sandy circles from Museum to Genuine Maasai Village, his toes chalky inside the tire sandals, heels white from dust and callus.

Behind me, the guard says I'm not me, this horse isn't mine, and I am not a cabman. I turn from you to respond with an arched, *Come Again?* brow, and he says, Whether you hit an owl with a stump or the stump with an owl, it's the owl who suffers. I smile diplomatically and ask, Where's a good place 'round here to eat?

At Vlad's Vodka House, you are the emaciated barmaid who calls herself a countess. She sits across from me over a beer-ringed tablecloth, linguine legs folded under her chin like a spring. She brought me six rounds of vodka On Zee House and said, I have six more rounds. Vant to see?

Russians plop O's from their mouths like teaspoons of caviar. O. Go. Go, says the Countess as she thrusts the butt of her .44 calibre into my palm. She clasps my wrist, guides the gun's muzzle up her throat, traces it along her lips, and plays Lifeguard, Mouth-To-Mouth. She says, You first. She says, Take a spin. Her breath reeks of pickled cabbage. I say, No, *nyet*. The barrel is long and dainty, the revolver older than Tsar Nicholas II. I say, What a handle! Is it walnut? Six cylinders, she says, one in six. I'm Not Scared. Go.

The pub is empty save the fat man counting cash and smoking cigarettes on a bar stool. The Union fell twenty years ago, but Vlad has yet to update the decor, the walls cluttered with portraits of Uncle Lenin and posters I can't read that shout Who Are You With and Workers Unite and Nowhere But Mosselprom. When the Countess grins, her lips stretch like the Neva River in an upside-down map of Petersburg. Coward, she says. My turn then. She flips the revolver in my hand so that the muzzle stares me in the third eye.

You and I had propped the card table five klicks west of Mission Harbour Station. We poured Earl Grey from the claw-footed pot of your mother's silver service. The tea party an ad hoc finale to the binge that followed our final finals of undergrad—rum gulped from globe glasses sharpied with rhumb lines, the twenty-sixer of Lemon Hart a cherry to top our two-scoop geography degree sundae. The loose leaf had oversteeped from the truck ride, but the tannins tasted familiar and vaguely reassuring. Truth or Dare, you had said after we ran out of rum, but if you choose Truth, you're a sissy. So we perched stiff and English, arrow spines, ankles crossed tidy, and we spoke in the Queen's tongue, in Henry Higgins, all Rain in Spain, How Now, Brown Cow—I asked for the sugar If You Please and you replied Of Course, My Squashed Cabbage Leaf. When the tracks trembled with the weight of the a.m. *Canadian* barrelling eastbound from Vancouver, we stared at ourselves in the reflections of one another's eyes, dared to sip tea when our ears buzzed with whistle. I blinked first, charged you and the table from the tracks—though in the end we had a good twenty seconds. Enough time for you to thumb a penny from your pocket and plant it on the rail.

And now my ears buzz with the Europop that leaks from the sound system, the mouth of the tsarist revolver pinned to the bridge of my nose. The backs of my arms prickle when the Countess lights a cigarette, and I realize that now the hand on the grip is my own. I close my eyes and see the city projected against my eyelids, a tourism montage: onion domes that blister jewels, cavernous ceilings painted with kings for kings, rearing bridges, rearing horses, all of it drenched in the ghoulish mirage of you.

Ruletka, the Countess says. Spin the cylinder. I push the thumbpiece until the chamber clucks open, roll the cylinder, and count holes until I find one with a bullet. Eyes closed, says the Countess, so I shut my lids and rotate the chamber back and forth with my thumb, trying to not track rounds. My palm folds the chamber back with a *click* and with a *click* I tap the hammer and squeeze the trigger and: *click*.

ARUSHA

At the centre of Africa between Cairo and Cape Town, a dove-haired woman sniffs mangoes from a wooden wheelbarrow. The vendor peels oranges with a machete and speaks to a woman shucking corn on the pavement beside her bowl of embers. Follows Her Nose wears high-waisted khakis and a white sleeveless blouse, and she looks like someone sixty who passes for forty-five, her cheeks slack without droop. I watch from my tin chair at the patisserie to see if she checks avocados like you, light squeeze in the palm of your hand. She does not.

Mount Meru looms over the city as crisp and conical as a bent elbow. A Maasai elder saunters up Sokoine with a gait steady enough to continue him north over the slope. Land Rovers and *dala-dalas* maelstrom 'round the roundabout—a herd of metal elephants, Carousel Africa on Stampede Speed. The murals on *dala-dala* windshields read like an atlas index: Hollywood, Jerusalem. Da Bronx. The elder is unfazed by the whirl of steel, our world of steel. As he threads through vehicles, his earlobes swing like balance balls. A Rover barrels behind him and I lose sight until he arrives whole on the other side. He hoods his blanket over his head and ambles away under a canopy of sidewalk trees.

At the primary school in Mianzini I sit opposite the headmistress with clouds in her hair. She lounges in a donated recliner, seventies velvet stretched over cushion like grafted skin. Her girl aerosols the cloud from an aluminum can, massages puffs into the black nest of her weave. She looks queenly in a burgundy pantsuit, luminous and rotund, buxom cheeks and eyes that chirp. Sit, she says, take bites and chai. After a flutter of Swahili a second girl sails into the office with a blue Thermos and donuts, umbrella-patterned *kitangi* knotted around her waist. She stirs my tea and plugs the wet spoon back into the sugar bowl. Outside the screen door, a wire-haired baby rolls in the gravel with a newborn pup. Her giggles rise into the banana leaves like bubbles inside a glass bottle of Fanta. Last time, you sat beside me, and I remember you drank Fanta instead of chai because you thought the carbonation might Do Your Stomach Good, like ginger ale, because you felt a Touch Queasy, and I remember that the Fanta haloed your lips orange. Headmistress says, *Pole, pole sana*, which means she is sorry, very sorry for my loss, or her country's mosquitoes, or your distaste for repellent, the way it made your palms so sticky-like-skin-under-Band-Aids, or for my cod liver cheeks, the grey bags beneath my eyes.

In the room we rented on Fire Road, I dragged our bed onto the balcony because your muscle joints could brand cows, because inside was too, too, too, too, because the oxygen between walls clogged your throat. Seven p.m. and the sun on its way to the other side of the world, sub-equator sky as unfamiliar as a friend after a car crash, stars scrambled like dice. Yahtzee. The stone pillars of the front gate were spiked with broken bottle glass, amber and green triangles that glinted with the occasional sweep of the guard's flash-light. Your head in my lap, hair like an oil spill, wet black knots splayed across my thigh. I cheered you with puns. Your cheeks hot, eyelids a-flutter. A map is like a fish because they both have scales. You don't have to understand everything about geographic information systems, as long as you get the GIS of it. How do geographers find the girl they're going to marry? They datum.

I fingered through your knots, memorized the curls, calculated the angles between cowlicks. Your hair streamed in kinks, black rivers that wound east and west and north from your skull, two centimetres above scalp level. Lush plains, low elevations, save the downy helices that corkscrewed from the coast of your ear. I wanted to preserve you, to shade you from direct sunlight, store you in optimal humidity within an acid-free frame. I wanted to make you a legend.

Slimebank Taxonomy

On Gin's first trip to the slimes, she found a fox. She could tell by its ears, how they arced from the tailings, and its chin, fine boned, jaw shellacked open. Three points suspended in misshapen geometry, a tranquility so malformed she sprinted home for a net—sprinted in case it was still sinking, through rows of white birch and winter-dead roses, toward the frozen slush that led to their cabin. She used her nephew's butterfly catcher because none of them fished, a sturdy wide one her brother brought from Papua New Guinea. She returned with it, a milk jug of water, and rubber gloves in case the oil was corrosive. When she dipped the hoop into the pond, the mesh trailed behind like a wise man's beard in a bowl of grey soup. Though hardly larger than a terrier, the shape sagged in the net and tripped Gin forward when she yanked it toward her. Dregs slid from its spine in webs, the pelt so slick she couldn't discern single hairs—only a glossy mat up the flank, textured like the implied fur of ceramic cats.

She and Clare had arrived at her brother's last month. The exile recommended by her doctor after a week of sleep, deficient lactation, and not wanting to nurse even with formula. Pink pills, blues tests. *I do not feel sad. I feel sad. I feel sad all the time and cannot snap out of it.* The usual surveys. "Inventories," they call them. As though smiles were merchandise. The complete stock shelved on her lips—one for the custodian, one for the nurse. Sorry, Doc, fresh out. They moved her from Maternity to Psychiatrics on day three. The nurse had clucked into the room to find Clare shrieking in her lap, Gin watching, arms limp at her sides, her eyes exploring her daughter as they might a photograph in a coffee-table book. Coarser nurses in Psychiatrics. Paintings of sand dollars. Clare slept downstairs with the gelatinous mauve elephants. More tests. Scales. *I have laughed: as much as I always could. Not quite so much now. Definitely not so much now.* Do Re Mi. Never a Rorschach—too clichéd, perhaps, but too bad, because that's one she might have enjoyed. She liked to divine images from shadows—from points on a dead fox's head. Ear to nose to ear, the lines she wiped first. A *V* fingered into the bitumen, Cassiopeia folded in half.

She hailed from Vancouver, a glass city where the sun shone 360 degrees: sky to sea to the condos on Coal Harbour. She hadn't liked it much, but this Syncrude hinterland was by all accounts a hole. Even with the thaw, the collapse of icicles into the underbrush. The fragrance of peat moss and bird breath and other springtime anomalies. She ventured outside the night her baby stopped wailing and her sister-in-law's voice sugared through the cedar planks. First she sat upright and listened, poised in the centre of her bed. Goodnight, stars. Goodnight, air. Goodnight, noises everywhere. Then she slid into her brother's sheepskin slippers and slipped the hell out—flannel sheet limp around her shoulders and enough sub-horizon sun reflected from the snow that she didn't need a flashlight.

Her limbs were bed stiff, baggy with three weeks' inactivity, but her paralysis wasn't physical. There was less snow beneath the roses and the birds had left a few frostbitten hips, strange spidered fruit latched to the branches in lattices of ice. The pond drew her because it was the only thing not frozen. An alien crater behind the birch, the bitumen floating in coagulated mats as skim might on a tub of tepid gravy. Now she crouched on the gravel, milk jug almost emptied, fox corpse as clean as she could get it. The forest blocked the sun, but her shadow on the slush suggested it had risen. She laid the fox on the shrinking patch of snow that capped a white stump and palmed its fur so that all the hairs pointed the right way. Its paws were bent in paddle, its lips lifted over the gums. Up the bank, two white-throated sparrows skittered from shrub to shrub, their songs tinny in the echo of upriver dump trucks and draglines. She leaned the butterfly net against the stump, collected her milk jug, and followed the birch trees home.

The silence felt like night when she slipped through the door. Lights still off, blinds pulled. She tracked wet onto the front mat and removed her slippers, the slush melting into fast puddles, her feet swollen and stinging onto the hemp weave. She saw a turtle-ish hulk breathing in the green glow of the wall night light. Her nephew hunched in the hall beneath a tangle of bedsheets, as though he tried to shove them behind his back when she opened the door. They stared at each other, both pegged to their corners, Jake all linen and eyelashes and trying to stand straighter, to hide the bedding with his sixty-pound frame. Gin lowered her eyes and leaned the door closed with her shoulder. Her own blanket coiled wet and tarry between her feet. She stepped off the mat and he moved too. When they passed each other, she glanced to find his eyes on the hardwood, until he stepped through the kitchen to the room with the washer and she sank behind her own four walls.

Her brother knocked on her door an hour later, all suited up in company coveralls, scalp a few inches shy of the door frame.

"Hey," he said.

She tugged the blanket to her chin and stared at a knot in the wall.

"Gamelle's taking Clare and Jake to the pool in town if you want to go. Jake has swimming."

"Thank you, no," she said, and shut her eyes.

She heard the cedar creak beneath him as he shifted his weight. "Right," he said. "Well, there's coffee in the kitchen."

She waited for his boots to plunk down the hall and out the door until she rooted in her suitcase for wool socks. Then she rolled them over her chapped damp toes and climbed out of bed.

Jake stooped at the table with a bowl of Cheerios milk and an anime comic. When Gin sat opposite him, he scanned up the tablecloth and adjusted the goggles he wore strapped to his forehead.

"Jake, can you check the formula?" Gamelle shouted from down the hall.

He lifted his bowl with both hands and tipped it into his mouth.

"Jake?"

"Minute," he called, milk dribbling down his chin.

The silhouette of a bottle orbited the microwave and a pot of oats boiled on the stove. Gin could see the porridge from her seat, a single gummy mass that bloated up the sides of the pot. She shifted her eyes to the microwave as it blacked and started dinging.

"Jake, the formula," called Gamelle as she tore into the kitchen, red hair flailing from the elastic, stained towel flung over her shoulder, and Gin's baby hitched to her hip. "Oh," she said when she saw her at the table.

Gin averted her eyes back to the porridge pot when Clare squirmed in Gamelle's arm, pinched faced and blotchy, screaming. The microwave dinged. Jake slurped milk from his bowl. The oats loomed in a perfect dome above the rim. Clare shrieking. Jake wiping the milk off his mouth with his sleeve. The porridge hissing in a slow wave onto the stove.

"Fuck," said Gamelle as she glanced over her shoulder. She wiped the sweat off her cheek with her free arm and snatched the formula from the microwave. "Jake, clean up the porridge."

"But, Mom—"

"Or no swimming." Her housecoat flared at her heels as she stormed back into the hall.

That night she found ducks. Two of them, tail up in tailings like an ironic postcard. A third tarred to its side, single patch of iridescent jade sheening from its neck under the beam of her flashlight. She had left in the early blue hour, with boots this time, a toothbrush, and another jug of water. They were easy to miss, there yesterday for all she knew. She netted two in one go and weaved the hoop back through the sludge for the third, the mud funnelling from the bottom when she lifted the net into the air, casting slow circles toward the shore. She dumped the ducks on the bank where her fox draped the stump, fur whited by frost, an icicle slanting off the tip of its tail.

Snow seeped through her nightgown when she sat, eventually numbing her rear so she couldn't feel any gravel. She scooped a duck with her glove and started at the bill—rubbed the slick with soft toothbrush strokes, inching between its eyes. Both wings were stretched from the body, like at any moment the bird might vault from her hand, tail feathers beating her chin in a tar-heavy tumble into the sky. She poured water from the jug and wiped its head with her thumb until she hit green, focusing on the bills and necks and feet because the feathers were too matted and too easily tugged out. Then she laid her ducks by size in a row—the idiom toppled by their ghoulishness: bodies half tarred, an odd wing snapped ninety degrees, ankles stretched like Chinese window poultry. But they were lined in order and she could see their faces.

The next evening she sat in the bay of the den window with the *Birds of Alberta*. Her brother was streaming hockey in his room with the baby, and Gamelle had driven to Fort McMurray to pick up the PAC ladies and donuts. Gin knew her ducks were mallards, but she liked to read the trivia—how their iridescence is called a "speculum," and how female ducks quack loudest. Even more, she liked the shape of Latin on her tongue. *Anas platyrhynchos*, like broken glass, sherry shards pressed to the roof of her mouth. The categorization of every beast through accordioning syllables. *Anas clypeata*. The Northern Shoveller. Close to a mallard, but with bills shaped like spoons and males that say *wook wook wook*.

"Want to see my favourite?"

Jake hovered at her elbow in insect pyjamas. Praying mantises or grasshoppers scattered up his chest.

"It's on page 167."

She didn't know how to respond so she thumbed to the page.

"The Sandhill Crane," he said, and climbed onto the arm of the couch.

"Grus canadensis." She gathered her dusty blond hair into a twist down the side of her nightgown collar. "Why do you like it?"

"They fly through here around this time. And when they stand in the yard, they look like statues." He lifted his arms and tested his balance, nudging his toe up the couch's brown leather.

"He's handsome," she said, and peered out the windowpane. Women's voices and cocktail laughter trickled in from the porch.

"Just Mom's friends," said Jake when she snapped the book shut. "Her turn for pickup." He leaped off the couch and landed with a thudded squat, then marched into the front hall as though Gin might want proof.

She glanced at the wall that divided the hall from the den and listened for the door to fling open to a pack of flapping tongues. Waited for the women to stomp into the hall, to find her in the window—their sour-sweet smiles as they say, *So you're Ginny.*

She pressed her shoulder blades against the wood of the alcove and drew her feet up the sill, flattened her chest to the front of her thighs.

"Jake, what are you doing up," said Gamelle. She herded him from the front hall to the kitchen, where Gin couldn't see. "Go brush your teeth."

Coated figures filtered in the same direction. One woman paused at the den, leaned into the door frame for balance as she removed her boots. Gin shallowed her breath and waited to be noticed—the woman wavering on a nyloned foot and tugging at her plastic spiked heel.

"It's only eight o'clock," Gin heard Jake say from the kitchen. "Plus I can't find my toothbrush."

The woman in the doorway straightened, wet boot in each hand. She stared into the den, hair framing her cheeks in tidy blond parentheses, her eyes poring up and down the wall adjacent to Gin's window.

"Is that Spanish Olive in your living room?" she said as she turned from the doorway and followed the ladies into the kitchen. "We considered it for the sunroom, but in the end we went with the Tourmaline."

Gin exhaled, her breath warming the tops of her knees. She listened to the clatter of the coffee pot, and then her baby as she started screaming from the room at the end of the hall.

"Oh, she'll probably need changing," said Gamelle from the kitchen. "Sit. Help yourself to Timbits."

She heard the bedroom door open and close. The crying subsided.

"Poor thing," said a woman in the kitchen.

"Both of them," said another woman.

"I heard they sent her from Vancouver."

"Guess Dad's not in the picture."

"Probably buggered off."

"Could you pass a Dutchie?"

Gin folded her chest back to her thighs. Her breasts ached. She ignored the damp as it cooled through her dressing gown cotton—a thin grey seep not quite like milk.

That night she counted in nursery games. Duck, duck, duck, goose. A Canada goose, to go by the cheek patches, though the mud obfuscated the feather schemes. Its wings were spread, but webbed by the bitumen, its neck stretched 180 degrees. So far all the birds were migratory, and she wondered if it had something to do with pond temperatures. This dark hole punctuating white fields, white lakes, white trees like a blinking motel sign on the highway to Fort McKay. A warm mouth to rest your wings in after a continental flap. She imagined the sludge to have a mummification quality, her pond dwellers preserved like the corded wood people inside Nordic bogs. Duck, duck, duck, goose, fox. Fowl of the air, beast of the fields, her slimebank taxonomy.

At home she lay on her bed and whispered verses of *Goodnight Moon* to her sunken belly like back in month three. She had been a model mother then. Single, but fresh eyed and rosy, dreaming girls' names and bedspreads and invigorated by the life inside her.

A wobbly voice interrupted her at the door.

"My butterfly net," he said. "What did you do to my net?"

She lifted her neck to watch Jake charge into her room, a gangly thing in blue underwear. He sprinted at the bed and tore off her top sheet, then stared down at her bare, stubbly legs.

She sat forward and covered her legs with her dressing gown.

"I was going to clean it," she said, which was true. She had carried it home to rinse off the tar and left it in the front hall umbrella stand for the night.

"My dad brought that net for *me* from the other side of the world." He stamped his foot on the *me*. "Not for you or your stupid baby." He stomped from the room and slammed her door on the way out. After a few minutes she heard the gush of the washing machine. And a few minutes after that, a gentle knock on his door. Gamelle's voice saying, "Jake?" Jake saying, "Go away." Gamelle saying, "Honey, what's wrong?" Jake saying, "Go away."

Gin lay there and watched the predawn shadows shift across her wall. Nights like these made her want to sleep with the window open so she could wake up with frost in her hair.

Early the next morning she hosed off Jake's net. It looked okay after the second round, grey but clean. She wrung out the netting and dripped inside to the bathroom. She dried the handle with a hand towel and the mesh with Gamelle's blow dryer. Jake was eating cereal in the den when she finished and slipped it inside his bedroom. She breezed back through the kitchen into the laundry room, found his sheets warm in the machine—he hadn't slept either, or else he woke early. She pulled them into a wicker basket and padded through the kitchen back to his room. Then she made his bed. Tucked the linen smooth and symmetrical beneath his mattress. Folded the top sheet over the quilt in a mint-worthy crease. She flattened the pillowcase with the palm of her hand, laid the butterfly catcher diagonally between the posts, and left to start a pot of coffee.

The baby cried most of the morning. Gin knelt at her bedroom wall with an empty mug and the bird book and listened to Gamelle try to coax the thing to sleep. Her tone would stiffen as the morning drew on, cradle song hissed instead of hummed: *Go to sleep, go to sleep little one ... oh god, just shut up and sleep*. Gin's knees were digging past the rug into the wood. They felt like they might be getting bruised. She pulled herself off the floor and went straight to the kitchen, found Jake standing with his nose pressed against the sliding glass door.

"Hi, Jake."

He turned with his finger to his lip, then beckoned her to the window.

Outside in the rose patch, two cranes drifted between thorns. Their tail plumes trailed in the snow, and though they needed to lift their knees to clear the brush, they strolled smooth as gospel, as souls drifting to the river to be dunked and declared saved.

"I shot one of those once," said Jake. He looked up at her, his big eyelashes. She hoped he never grew into them. "Well, my dad did. But he let me carry the gun."

"Why?" she asked, and examined the birds, how red feathered across their eyes.

"It was drowning in that black pond." He paused to glance at her again. "That's where you took my net, isn't it?"

She nodded, her eyes still planted outside.

"Well, thanks for cleaning it off." He opened the window and leaned out over the sill, the cranes' coos audible now, like softly rolled *r*'s. "My dad says they're supposed to use sound cannons to scare the animals, but that the pond doesn't exist because it's too small."

"Doesn't exist?"

"Not inside books."

"On the books?"

"Right," he said. They watched the cranes ghost into the underbrush. Ochre feathers like dusters, sweeping snow for the spiderwebs that hung beneath low-lying trees.

That evening they made a scarecrow. Jake searched his closet for clothes while Gin forged a torso—a broom and baseball bat trussed with duct tape into a cross. They dressed it in an Oilers jersey. No pants, due to lack of legs, but Jake volunteered a werewolf mask for the face. Gin's brother was working a double and wouldn't be home until late, so no one fussed about dinner. Gamelle emerged with Clare once to microwave formula and Alpha-Getti, a second time to ask what they were playing, and a third to suggest that Jake dial a friend. But mostly she kept to herself, as though she didn't want Clare and Gin in the same room. They decided to wait for daylight to raise the structure, so Jake crowned the effigy with a pink straw hat and settled with his father's laptop, while Gin returned to her bedroom wall.

Except she couldn't hear a thing. Or she could—the trills of cranes out the window, more of them now, and synthesized music from Jake's games, but not Clare—it occurred to her she hadn't cried for a while—and not Gamelle. So she left her room and stood at their door. Hovered her ear at the open crack and still heard nothing. She nudged the door open with her foot and found Gamelle folded on the bed, florid hair sprawled over the pillowcase. Bare feet and gently pocked forehead pointed to the ceiling, torso twisted so that her elbows could lie flat on the mattress to nest Clare, who slept cosseted in her blanket and sleeper gown.

"Aunt Gin, we need to go."

She turned to find Jake marshmallowed inside snow pants and a down jacket.

"What do you mean?" she whispered, and tugged the door closed.

"The cranes—there's a ton, or at least ten, and they're flying. Can you hear them? Listen, I can hear them. There's thousands and they'll land in the pond."

She raised her eyes to the ceiling as she listened. It did sound as though there were at least ten flying over the roof, cooing prettily, rolling their *r*'s.

"Hurry," said Jake as he waddled toward the front door, his snow boots tracking wet down the hall.

"Wait." She followed him, her sock feet landing in his boot puddles. "Shouldn't you check with your mother?"

"She's sleeping with your baby."

She glanced at Gamelle's bedroom door, then back to Jake. She straightened the nightgown off her hip bones. "Well, we'll need noisemakers."

"Noisemakers?" he said.

"Pots and spoons. Wooden spoons."

"Like New Year's."

"Right," she said, and moved into the kitchen to unhitch saucepans and soup pots from their hooks.

"I own a kazoo," said Jake, and he ran toward his room.

They met at the sliding glass door. Gin stepped into Gamelle's gumboots, no jacket because then she'd have to set down the pots, and Jake led the way out, stomped down the path to the rose thorns, scarecrow over his shoulder and red kazoo nearly falling out of his coat pocket. It was one of those small bright moons that blanched cheeks and silvered trees and cast all the shadows bigger. She could just make out the last pairs of hanging feet as the cranes soared above the birches. Two loomed in the clearing between the roses and the tree trunks, their bills cocked toward her and Jake as they plodded through the slush.

"Shoo," shouted Jake. He ran at the cranes, fumbled the kazoo from his pocket and pressed it to his lips.

Gin maintained her pace, bent her neck up to catch any birds in flight.

"Shout," said Jake. "Bang your pots. Here, I'll take some." He grabbed two from her pile so she could manoeuvre her hands, then sprinted into the woods.

"Crane, crane, go away," she sang softly, clanging together two saucepans. Then louder: "Don't come back another day."

She followed the kazoo toots through the trees until she spotted the scarecrow thrashing above Jake near the edge of the pond. The cranes circled overhead, their bodies suspended, coasting off the air without wing flaps. She banged a wooden spoon against her soup pot, just as she used to on December 31, hips bent over her Davie Street balcony rail.

"Happy New Year," she shouted as she jerked the spoon against the aluminum.

Jake laughed and yelled it too—"Happy New Year"—between metal clangs and bugles from his kazoo. "Happy New Year."

A solitary crane stood ankles-deep. He raised his wings at their approach, lurched back from the slickens, and lifted into the air. The others began to shriek and knot into a leggy cloud, some smacking neighbours with their wings. Gin beat her pot from where she stood on the bank and watched Jake run beneath them with the scarecrow, blaring his kazoo. The birds glided the way they came, the broomstick heaving at them from Jake's arms, pink straw hat hucked off now and floating in the pond.

"What is going on?" said Gamelle from the edge of the woods.

She stood at the trees in her bathrobe and a winter jacket that dangled unzipped at her thighs. She trudged toward Jake, nearly tripping over her half-on running shoes. "Are you out of your mind?" She stared at Gin, her eyes red rimmed.

"We're scaring the cranes, Mom."

When he turned to face her with the werewolf effigy, she stumbled backward and yelped, then recovered her balance with a palm in the air.

"I told you we were making a scarecrow," said Jake. He stepped toward her, enclosing her hand in his mitt. "Otherwise they'd have drowned. All those cranes—did you see?" he said, and folded inside his mother's jacket.

Gin searched the snow for something else to look at. Her eyes fell on her broken parade. The fox drooped off the stump, its limbs softer now. Some of her ducks were booted out of line by the commotion, their feathers spattered with kicked snow, eyes too dull to spot in the dark. It occurred to her they stank. The cold had delayed their decay, but the flesh was rotting now, and it mingled woozily with the stink of the oil.

"Oh," said Jake. "We lost one." He pointed toward the pond.

Next to the hat, a crane floated on its stomach with stretched legs and spread wings. Gamelle tilted Jake's chin away from the pond, hugged his cheek to her chest.

"I can't feel my hands," Gin mumbled as Gamelle smoothed the hood of Jake's coat. Neither of them seemed to hear her. "Maybe I'll go back."

"Is the crane dead?" Jake asked Gamelle. "Can we save him?"

Gin turned to face the woods as Jake suggested they fish the body out with the scarecrow pole. As Gamelle replied, "I don't know, sweetie." Then: "Is that my hat?"

She walked up the bank toward the thin white trunks and listened to her boot bottoms suck free from the thawing mulch. Their voices faded as she navigated the roses, her nightgown's wet hem slapping the backs of her knees, the thorns clinging to her collar, which flopped open as she trudged toward the house. She stamped up the wood stairs that led to the deck and stepped over the doorsill into the balmy thaw of the kitchen. She could hear Clare crying as she slid the door shut, stepped out of her gumboots, and breathed into her palms—this one the rhythm of half-hearted bursts that subsided whenever Gamelle entered the room to pick her up. She filled the kettle and set it on the stove, predicting the cry's pause and restart, higher pitched the second verse, almost a whistle. She leaned against the counter and waited for the water to boil, calculated Clare's next pause, the decrescendo. Then she followed the sound into the hall.

Clare lay tucked in the centre of the bed, her rosy eyelids clamped shut, forehead dimples scrunched toward the scoop of her nose in lieu of eyebrows. Gin lingered in the doorway until she heard Jake and Gamelle clomp into the house, heard Jake note the kettle and ask for hot chocolate. She nudged the door closed with her heel, and Clare stopped wailing long enough to blink at her. When she started again, it was the whistle rhythm, her mouth waxed open. The tears gathered in the dips beneath her eyes, and Gin watched how the lines graphed the curve of her cheek, eye to nose to lip. How they dripped off her chin and seeped white as radio static into the cotton collar of her nightgown.

We Walked on Water

Land of the misty giants. Cedar, alder, ponderosa pine. Cascade Mountains pushing out green like grass through a garlic press. The veg here is fungal. Jungle. Where am I—Thailand? I could be in Thailand. Bangkok, British Columbia. The Coquihalla. It's all rainforest: fern-webbed paths and moss like armpit hair, the exclusion of seventy per cent of the sky. You see the tallest trees in the first half of the drive—between home and Hope, Hope and Allison Pass. I'm the kid at the back of the bus with a packet of apple rings, slouched in his track pants over two velour seats. I could have cycled: Chilliwack to Penticton, 285 k, a hundred klicks longer than the route in the race. But it's best to not overdo it. Rest well, race well. Taper time now.

Aunt Bea will meet me at the terminal, in her plaid-patched skirts, smelling of patchouli. She'll drive her Volvo from Nelson—kayak on the roof rack when she rolls into the lot. Last year we "made a week of it." Our parents browsed bookshops and bead shops; Aunt Bea sat on the beach and sliced watermelon. Liv and I trained in the lake. We raced between the Peach and the Riverboat, and sometimes I let her win. Once she almost won for real, but I grabbed her heels and yanked her under. She kicked me in the hip and I let go. Asshole, she said. She splashed water into my eyes and swam to the shore to practise handstands.

When you train, numbers are everything. Kilojoules in and out, pounds per inch, the speed and duration of mass in motion. Zeros and ones, like a computer. Liv understood how to be a computer better than I did, though I think I've caught on. Our nutrition plans were similar: four to six small meals. Fistful of protein, fistful of starch, two fistfuls colour. We ate space food. Sports gels in squeeze tubes: Accelerade, Perpetuem. She dipped salted pretzels into cottage cheese. I drank nonfat chocolate milk.

What worried Mom was the swim scrum: one lake, no lanes. Anthem ends and the start horn blares. Twenty-six hundred participants wade into the water, identical in our neoprene and brightly coloured swim caps. It feels baptismal, sacrificial. We drop row on row into a tangle of leg and windmilling arms. Stay out of trouble, Liv, Mom said. Stay out of trouble. People assume she got held down. Five feet four inches, 105 pounds: easy to front-crawl over. But that wasn't it. She stayed nearby. The first leg, sixteen hundred metres lakeshore to Last House, I kept her in sight. In the scrum, you move as a group: collective consciousness, hive mind. Sometimes you let yourself be carried. You slip over bodies like spawning salmon, which Liv and I tried once. Salmon run 2005, Vedder River. We in our swim skins and matching caps. We let the current steer us. Watched their shadows through our goggles, how darkness darted over algaed stones.

Their hook jaws and front flared teeth, port-stain scales, how they tumbled over each other and over our ankles. The flick of their fins.

Last year, the swim started me off woozy. Three point eight kilometres, one breath per stroke cycle. Rhythm is key. Beats per minute, strokes per metre. Your heart, your lungs, your metronome. The left is my poor side. I breathed on my left for the first half of the course and on my right for the second. You learn how to swim slippery—when Liv and I practised at the pool, we took turns watching each other splash. Well, that was sloppy, she'd say. It's your legs. Your legs aren't straight. I would swim another length, and if it was better, she'd shoot a thumbs-up from the end of the lane.

Sometimes they wired separate music into the underwater speakers. You'd hear Top Forty on deck, but in the competition lanes, they played Beethoven. The lake is a different music—the calm white hum of underwater ear pressure. In the race, you follow that hum to the shore, then find your land legs, where your feet start and the wet sand ends. I remember juddering through the time chute—hands on my back, guiding me to the change tents. They unzip the wetsuit for you, spray you with sunscreen while you call for your glasses. I searched for Liv when I ran to the bike racks, but the ladies' tent was crowded and she always took longer to change. Some athletes would pause at the nutrient station. They peeled their bananas and PowerBar wrappers. I kept my bike calories in a single bottle. Accelerade + Carbo-Pro. Energy gels to top up.

Tonight Aunt Bea and I will eat spaghetti. I used to make fun of Liv when she measured, but this weekend I packed her food scales. Four hundred grams whole wheat spaghetti, crushed tomatoes, extra-lean turkey. After dinner, we'll drive the bike course. Follow the lakes: Skaha to Vaseux, Vaseux to Osoyoos. Penticton—Oliver—Keremeos, 180 kilometres. Every twenty-five klicks, I'll get out and cycle. That's how you notice the camber, the incline of road when the street appears flat. Never mind the mountain passes. The highest altitude comes near the end: twenty-five hundred feet. Aunt Bea will drive slow beside me. She will play Creedence Clearwater on tape. When she brakes for me to haul in the bike, she'll tell me she likes the way I walk, the way I talk. Tomorrow we'll drive the run route. We did this last year, but I don't like surprises. We all have our rituals. On race day, Liv used to eat sun. We have this skylight in our kitchen, and from May to September the light floods in. She'd stand below the glass with a bowl of white yogurt until the sun reeled off her spoon. I watched from the hall sometimes. You could pinpoint each moment the glare made her blink. But on Ironman Sunday you eat breakfast before sun-up. Check-in's at five; we set the radio for four. She aimed for toast and peanut butter, but couldn't keep it down. Race day nerves—I heard her retch in the shower. But ask any competitor: on race day you go liquid. Mothers said it in the fifties: don't eat and swim. A girl eats careful and it's a disorder; her brother eats careful and he's an athlete. We shared the same BMI.

This is the first time I've taken the Greyhound. Last year, our parents drove. Liv asked for lunch in Princeton because it was the only town with a Booster Juice. Booster Juice stamps the nutrition label on every drink, so you know you're getting thirty grams of protein with your five hundred calories of

Bananas-A-Whey. I wanted Dairy Queen. A Butterfinger Blizzard layered twice with hot fudge.

That's obscene, said Liv.

I have a craving.

That's over a hundred grams of sugar. For a medium.

Well.

Look at you. You'll make yourself sick. That's like six bananas.

How many bananas before you grow tits?

She didn't speak after that. She inserted her earbuds and frowned out the window. You knew Liv was upset if you saw a glimmer of sweat above her eyebrows, or on her cheekbones. And sometimes she left her mouth open after she spoke, like she couldn't quite catch her breath. But then I might poke her shoulder with my eyelids flipped inside out, and she would smack the back of my head.

Long QT syndrome, the medical examiner had said. Arrhythmia. Mutated sodium channels, reduced flow of potassium: the medspeak never sounded severe enough. This year, Mom forbade me to compete. She said that. She said, I forbid you. We fought when I registered in October, a few days before Halloween. We were carving pumpkins. She shoved hers off the counter with the heel of her palm.

Dad won't come this year either. He says it's because of work, but he's not contracted for Sundays. Last year, they ate at Thomasina's, a bakery with oven-hot scones and rounds of sourdough that steam from the centre when you pry them in half. We all shared a booth. Liv and I plugged into our iPods and frosty wax cups. Mom and Dad staring out the window, buttering their scones.

I think the tallest building in Princeton is the Visitor Information Centre. My bus waits there thirty minutes, and I might treat myself to a Strawberry Slam. Sometimes I wonder about the diets of other animals. How millennia of worms and wood bugs might contribute to the bone density of birds. The musculature of flight, lean protein for air-friendly pectorals. Versus penguins, which swim and eat squid. We've lost weight since we were apes; we've become more aerodynamic. I wish we had wings. Though the run rules say *no form of locomotion other than running, walking, or crawling*. Liv cut that line from the athlete guide and pasted it into her journal. It was funnier before the bike-to-run transition. The weight of your muscles, the downward propulsion, your blood and your breath pumping into the pavement.

Last year I made it to dusk. To the chicken broth and Coca-Cola. The Coke fizz went down like static electricity, like the charge from a balloon you rub in your hair and stick to the wall. The volunteers distributed the broth in warm paper cups. You would ease into a jog and graze fingers with the kid in a mint volunteer shirt as he handed you the cup. The broth tasted like the most nourishing thing you'd had all day, and you held the liquid in your cheeks and nodded at the kid, who had Down's syndrome, and he grabbed another cup from the table and fired you an A-okay sign.

At one point near Skaha Estates, I stopped running at the top of a hill and waited forty-five seconds to spot Liv. I thought she must be ahead of me. She was a stronger runner. I thought maybe she slipped in front when I used the toilet at the bike-to-run. But then I saw Dad's Ford Escape at the turnaround on Christie Beach and his cheeks slanted white through the windshield. Athletes crowded the special needs table, ghosted the nutrient station with their neon bottles of Gatorade. I stalked off the road and walked straight to the car. He shifted his eyes to me through the window, and for a moment neither of us moved. He flicked a switch at the wheel and the passenger door unlocked. I opened the door and climbed into the front seat and his palm clapped my shoulder. His eyes squinted into mine, and then he turned the ignition. I noticed there were two small Tim Hortons coffees in the cupholders. He drove off the course, on the other side of Skaha Lake, and it wasn't until we were halfway to Kaleden that he pointed to the cup nearest me and said, That one's yours.

A premature ventricular contraction is medspeak for *your heart skips a beat*. The contraction is initiated by your heart ventricles rather than the sinoatrial node. You can listen to a high-pitched recording on Wikipedia. It sounds like bagpipes. *Tempo rubato* is Italian for stolen time. Rhythmic freedom. The expressive speeding up and slowing down of a piece of music. Chopin played steady with his left hand, timed to the metronome, while his right hand weaved in and around the beat like a ferret inside a chest of drawers. Your left is your clock. Your timekeeper. Liv played Chopsticks with her toes. Tilted onto her tailbone, the stool pushed back, half a grapefruit between her palms. She sucked the juice through a straw, and I waited for her to flick her chin and fire the pulp at me. I remember her in screenshots. Like she's in motion, but my mind can only capture single frames. That's how I imagine her in the lake. Involuntarily, when my mind slips in flashes. Liv with her jaw gaped, gasping in water. Liv with a thin wrist braced to her thorax. Liv with her eyes bulged like a fish. When I imagine my sister, I do not see Ophelia. Her heart's seized and she's choking in lake, and I wonder at what point she knew.

I read once that grief is like waiting. Waiting to sleep. Waiting to wake up. Waiting for Act III, the plot twist. Like when you drop a twig into the stream and it never emerges on the other side of the bridge. Tonight in Penticton, I might take out Bea's kayak. Go for a paddle. Liv and I rowed the swim course last year, with a Thermos of hot chocolate and a box of Ritz crackers, our boom box, the Beach Boys, and six D batteries. We paddled into that warm darkness, the blue hour of bats. How they screeched and swooped over the dry-patched Summerland hills. Liv laid her oar across the cockpit coaming and shut her eyes. I continued to row. Motel neon glowed from the lakeshore, and we slipped past their spears of reflected light.

ACKNOWLEDGMENTS

Versions of these stories appeared in the following publications: "Who Will Water the Wallflowers?" in *The Walrus*; "Ship's Log" in *The Malahat Review*, *Journey Stories 22*, and *Elbow Room*; "My Sister Sang" in *Grain*, *Journey Stories 25*, and *Coming Attractions 12*; "L'Étranger" in Hazlitt and on CBC Canada Writes; "Nightwalk" in *Descant*; "Where have you fallen, have you fallen?" in *The Vancouver Review* and *Journey Stories 24*; "Roadnotes" in *PRISM International* and *Coming Attractions 12*; "Worried Woman's Guide" in *The Fiddlehead*; "Missing Tiger, Camels Found Alive" in *The Indiana Review*; "Sea Life" in *Little Fiction*; "Thoughts, Hints, and Anecdotes Concerning Points of Taste and the Art of Making One's Self Agreeable: A Handbook for Ladies" in *Prairie Fire*; "Good for the Bones" in *Room*; "Here Be Dragons" in *The New Quarterly* and *Coming Attractions 12*; "Slimebank Taxonomy" in *Willesden Herald New Short Stories 6*; and "We Walked on Water" on *Granta*'s New Writing. Thank you to all the editors.

Most of this book was written under the guidance and green thumbs of faculty at the University of Victoria. Thank you John Gould, Steven Price, Bill Gaston, and Lorna Jackson, who taught my first fiction class when I still wanted to be a lawyer. Thank you also to Jean McNeil, Henry Sutton, Giles Foden, and Andrew Cowan at the University of East Anglia.

Resounding thanks to my peerless agent, Karolina Sutton, who took me on at the risk of cementing her reputation as a one-woman orphanage for story writers. And thank you to all three of my editors: Nicole Winstanley, Rachel Mannheimer and Helen Garnons-Williams. I am lucky to work with a team of such exemplary women. Thank you also to my transatlantic publicists: Stephen Myers, Anthony LaSasso and Madeleine Feeny. Indeed, thank you everyone behind the pages at Hamish Hamilton and Bloomsbury. I know it took a lot of hands to produce this book.

I would like to thank my workshop pals at UVic and UEA, and someone who was never a workshop pal, but my arch rival, Dave. Dub, I have ridden your flannel coattails across the Atlantic. Without your meddling, my life would look very different. You are an important friend.

Most of all, I owe this collection to my father, John, my mother, Kathryn, and my brother, Jesse. If you were any more supportive, you would be writing these stories yourselves. (Once or twice you have tried.) I am grateful for you. Dad, you were my most ardent reader. I can see you in every page.